Revenge o

By Paul F. Smith

1
The Butter Cross Murder

It was 7.30am on Wednesday 13th April 1966 Detective Superintendent Ralph Renton was day off he was sitting in his kitchen eating breakfast and leafing through yesterdays Yorkshire Post. Despite it being a day off he couldn't get out of the habit of up showered and shaved and breakfast by 7.30am. Jenny his partner sitting opposite him said "We must sort out our engagement party time is marching on."

He was just about to answer her when the telephone in the hall rang as he picked up the receiver he instinctively looked at his wristwatch.

"Hello Ralph"from his accent Renton knew it was his detective inspector Frank Dipper "Sorry to spoil tour day off but a local bobby has found a body very dead at Hooton Pagnell sprawled across the butter cross and it is in our boundary. Doctor Wells is on his way as his Peter Johns I can pick you up in ten minutes."

Renton said "Righto see you then."He walked back into the kitchen and Jenny said "Don't tell me that is our day together out of the window I don't suppose I will see you until tonight?"

Renton said "We have plenty of time to organise it and let's have a big family and friends bash here, the house is more than big enough."
She said "Something special I was thinking about Italy."

"I will brush up on my Italian senora or is that signora?"

"Very funny."

Just then a car horn sounded outside it was Frank Renton kissed Jenny and then went outside and got in the car.

Renton said "Where is Hooton Pagnell?"

"It is a small hamlet on the B6422 between here and South Elmsall the road in the hamlet is quite narrow and a bit of a chicane as you will see the body is male and apparently his head is hanging on with just a bit of skin."

They left Doncaster and drove into the countryside with a couple of houses here and there as the mist began to thin out eventually the road began to climb. They came to a very high grand wall made from local stone then went into the chicane through high walls and then ahead they could see the butter cross and Peter Johns taking photographs. Peter was the dedicated fingerprint officer and in later years would be known as a SOCO.

Frank stopped the car near the cross let Renton out and then parked the car away on the other side of the road. Renton walked to the wall and looking over it there was a 30 feet drop to the lane below and now that the early morning mist was clearing he could see in the distance the winding gear for Frickley pit and the village.

The body was sprawled across the lower step of the plinth with the head pointing to the wall there was a lot of blood on the steps of the plinth and towards the wall.

Doctor Wells walked from his car and looked at the body and said "Not a pleasant death he knew he was going to die."

Renton said "Why do you say that Doc?"

"Looking at him from here I would say he was garrotted but I will be able to say after the post mortem, my chaps will be here soon and I will get them to wash this blood away. Looking at the blood I would say this happened last night."

Just then the mortuary team arrived and placed the body in the usual wooden box and after a word with the doctor and finding an outside tap nearby they used several buckets to wash the blood towards the drain.

Renton said to Peter "Can you take a couple of photographs from the end of the chicane towards the butter cross?"

"Yes sir." Peter said.

Renton then walked towards Frank who was talking to a uniformed bobby.

Frank said "This is PC Hartwell he is one of the local coppers from South Elmsall." The constable saluted.

Renton shook his hand and said "I understand you found the body what time was that?"

"7am sir I start at 6am and cycle up here every morning Hooton Pagnell is on the edge of my beat. I check all the farm gates on the way up because children like to leave them open and let the cow's out."

"Did you see anyone about?"

"No sir only the 7.30 bus coming through from Doncaster."

"If you can write out a statement and I will get someone to pick it up?"

"Very good sir will do."He then saluted and cycled off towards South Elmsall.

Renton said to Frank "do you know the corpse?"

"Yes Eric Cooper, from Doncaster, drinker and scrapper, he was arrested at Christmas for urinating on the Town Hall steps and made the mistake of taking a swing at Sergeant Ramsden."

Renton said "As my local guide what can you tell me about this area?"

This had become a standing joke between them because Frank had been raised in the Doncaster area.

"It's in the Domesday Book got a Royal Charter in the 13th Century which meant they could hold a market on a Thursday and have a fair which is usually in July. The school here usually has about 8 pupils and Mrs Kelly gives them one to one education most of the kids go to the grammar school in Doncaster. The village was owned by William St Andrew Warde Aldam and a lot of their money came from the pits."

"What about policing round here?"

"Hartwell is one of four constables that police the villages around here from South Elmsall to Ackworth, South Kirkby, Badsworth and Skelbrooke. Their sergeant is Samuel "Smudge" Smith ex pit blacksmith and fitter bit of a character and few offenders make it to court he dispenses justice in his own way and it works. His mentor was Sergeant Austin Bradley and also his Godfather."

Renton and Frank then returned to the police station and went to the collators office where the murder investigation room would be set up. The collators office had a card system which in later years would be replaced with computers. Thousands of cards with the names of proven criminals and the unproven relating to Doncaster and the surrounding areas that came under their jurisdiction. Presiding over this office was PC Reg Prestleigh famous for his magnificent quiff and impersonations of Elvis.

Back in the collators office Frank made a mug of coffee for Renton and a very strong mug of tea for himself.

Renton said "Reg here is one pound for the murder tea fund and could you set up the boards table and chairs ready for briefing at 11am.I will see appraise the Chief at morning prayers but give Jack Bradley and Steve Bowers a call to come in, the dead man is a Eric Cooper what can you tell me about him?"

"Yes he was last nicked at Christmas, born in Hooton Pagnell, mum was visiting a cousin. The family live in Armthorpe he still lives there with mum. Dad died 10 years ago in a pit accident."

"Married?"

"Once, it lasted several months, but when she found out his one true love was the pub, she left him and now has found a better man and lives in York."

"Job?"

"Worked for the council as a dustman and road sweeper any odd jobs they needed doing."

Frank said "Why kill him in such a public place, on the main bus route as well?"

Reg said "Perhaps that's where they met or ended up or maybe the killer is making a statement."

2
Morning Prayers

Wednesday
13th April 1966

10.45am Renton walked out of the new Chief's office and down to the murder room.

Frank passed Renton a mug of coffee, "How was morning prayers?"

"Present was Sergeant Ramsden, Chief Inspector Rogers, Chief Inspector Johnny Martin and worst of all Walter Benson."

Walter Benson was the Chairman of the Watch Committee or as they became to be known as the Joint Planning Committee. Benson's nickname by certain police officers was "Kipper" two faces and no guts, but others called him Doubting Thomas.

"I thought he had retired, what's happened to Henry Sykes?" said Frank.

"On holiday hiking somewhere."

The new Chief had been in office for nearly a year but as far as his officers were concerned he had a lot to prove yet compared to the old Chief. He had been a Superintendent in another Force and had not served in the Armed Forces.

"Benson was his usual self, he tried to tell the Chief how a murder investigation should be conducted, but the Chief put him firmly in his place, Benson then left because he had another meeting to attend to apparently. The Chief did say that we could have Jack, Steve, Dennis Parkin and Tina Shaw for a start. Johnny Martin will give us constables to do the house to house shouldn't take too long in a hamlet Steve will be the DS.

Several minutes later they all trooped in followed by Austin Bradley, Jack's dad. Although a retired uniform sergeant he still popped in to see Reg and was useful for his local knowledge.

When they were all seated and had made a drink for themselves Reg stood up rattling the tea caddy.

"Inspectors and above pay one pound" he rattled the tin at Frank "The rest of you it is 10 shillings per month or anything up to sixpence for a mug."

"Thank you Reg" said Renton he continued "Body found at the butter cross in Hooton Pagnell by the local bobby Pc Hartwell at 7am.The victim had a very large gash from ear to ear almost severing his head .According to Doc Wells he was probably garrotted with wire we will know more after the post mortem and I am sure he will explain it all in his inimitable fashion. The 7.30am bus had gone past the passengers will have got a good look and will set tongues wagging I am sure. Over to you Reg."

"Yes Eric Cooper spinster of our parish known I am sure to all of you born 5th August 1934 actually in Hooton Pagnell, Mum was visiting a cousin like you do when you are heavily pregnant. The Cooper family then was Eric and his mum and dad at the time, dad died in a pit accident 1956 mum still lives in Armthorpe. Drinker and scrapper last arrested on Christmas Eve for urinating on the Town Hall steps and for taking a swing at Ted Ramsden silly boy."

Renton said "Jack and Tina can you go and see dear old mum break the sad news to her and have a look around the house. Dennis can you take Austin to the council yard I am sure Austin will have a contact there find out when they last saw Cooper and did he ruffle any feathers enemies all that stuff right lets go for it back here at 4pm for a debrief also we will be keeping a diary of all our movements from now on and the file will be here on the table next to the collators desk once we have various statements and the pm report it will be here for you all to read."

Renton then telephoned the mortuary.

"Yes Ralph" said Doctor Wells "Definitely garrotted with a double wire I would say bruising in his back where the killer pushed his knee as he pulled his head back with the wire very professional."

"Did you say a double wire, why?"

"Well actually it is one wire wrapped round the neck twice. If the victim managed to get his hand on one of the wires to pull it away from his throat he would then simply tighten the second wire."

"Professional you said?"

"This technique was perfected by the French Foreign Legion. Time of death I would now say was between 3am to 4am."

"So why kill him there in such a public place?"

"At 3am there would have been no-one there, the buses finish at 11pm and I think the killer is saying "I am here look out" a warning to someone else maybe and once the first bus comes pass everyone on the bus would have seen the body and the blood and tongues will be wagging as we speak."

"4pm will be a debrief."

"I will try to make it."

Renton said "Johnny Martin has got together 6 constables and they are being transported to Hooton Pagnell to do house to house or is that farm to farm. Detective Officer's Tinsley and Sykes will be with them to take any statements. If they get anything really important they will ring Reg who will contact me or Frank see you all later."

3
Berlin

Wednesday
13th April 1966
4pm Debrief

Renton said "Jack and Tina what did mum have to say about the demise of her lovely son?"

"Not a lot." said Tina "She was upset and said she was all alone now."

Jack said "She omitted to mention all the times he had threatened her when he was drunk."

Tina continued "She said she knew drink would be his downfall and after he received the letter he drank even more, which was about 6 weeks ago."
Tina passed the letter to Renton. He opened it and pulled out a note and what looked like a cardboard badge. The note had written on it "Hello Eric hoping I can get to see you and the others, mate". It wasn't signed the badge consisted of a black dot about the size of a penny inside a red circle, at the top of it was the word BERLIN.

Renton said "Hmm very strange what do you think Austin?"

Austin Bradley the father of Jack Bradley had served in the Royal Marine Light Infantry in World War One and was a bit of a buff on all things military.

"It's the badge of the Berlin Infantry Brigade. They were part of the infantry along with the Yanks who guarded the perimeter between West and East Germany and onwards after the building of the Wall. The French were there also but they had a different name for it of course. Three thousand soldiers in total in various barracks".

Steve said "Checkpoint Charlie and all that Cold War stuff."

"Yes that was mainly the Redcaps the military Police at Checkpoint Charlie were very strict."

Jack said to Steve "Didn't you do National Service then Steve?"

Steve said "Yes I got Kenya thank you not a nice place to be in 1956."

Austin continued "The Berlin Infantry Brigade was borne out of a force called Area Troops Berlin. Of course National Service provided a useful source of men and they were trained specifically for that task. Also the Suez Crisis popped up, in some areas they were called gunfodder. I am sure Steve knows what that means".

Renton said "So did mum say that Cooper changed after the arrival of the letter?"

"She said that he had come into some money, she didn't know where probably from the racecourse and he did start drinking more and seemed more worried in his sober moments."

"Austin how did you and Dennis get on at the council yard?"

"Well between us I reckon we know everyone that works there. They said he was a good worker when he was there. He spent most of his time pushing a dustbin on wheels sweeping the street and would fill in on the dustcart during the holiday season. He did call in sick about a week ago and that happened occasionally."

"Righto, Tina when did mum last see him?"

"Yesterday he left home in time for the pubs opening."

"Did he have a favourite watering hole?"

"Any pub that was open, but he did go to South Elmsall occasionally to meet a mate called Gerry, she didn't know his surname a miner apparently they had both started at Frickley pit as trainees."

"Righto, tomorrow Jack and Austin have a sniff around South Elmsall see if you can track Gerry down and which pubs they met in. Steve and Tina pubs in Armthorpe and Doncaster see who he met there, any regulars. Reg what about Coopers National Service record and who he served with. The doc said he would be here if he could so let's have another brew and give him a bit more time."

After everyone had made a drink and settled down in walked Doctor Wells.

"Hello chaps and you madam," Tina visibly blushed.
Jack said to Steve "What an old charmer."

Doctor Wells continued "The victim died somewhere between 3 and 4am where he was found. He had quite a bit of alcohol in his stomach and a bruise in his lower back. He was garrotted using a double wire that is one wire wrapped around his neck and then pulled backwards as his killer used his knee to push him forwards hence the bruising in his back. Even if Cooper had managed to get his hand on one wire he would then be tightening up the second wire. The type of garrotte with the double wire was perfected by the French Foreign Legion. I would suggest that the killer was a pro and probably has done this before. With his head almost severed from his body he would have bled to death in minutes. The shock alone would have killed him."

"So why in Hooton Pagnell?" Jack said.

"He wants the attention of someone, I surmise it is a warning to others maybe when it is featured in the newspapers and don't forget the early bus went past at 7.30 am so tongues will be wagging causing rumours. Death at the Butter Cross sounds like a murder novel. What."

He paused and then said "Must dash chaps see if my horse came in."

As the doctor left Renton said "You all know what you are doing tomorrow I will see you all at the 4pm debrief.

Just then David Tinsley walked in.

Renton said "David what have you got."

"Not a lot Hooton Pagnell dies every day when the Post office closes and by 11pm when the last bus goes through then it becomes asleep until the local constable arrives in the morning. However one chap Alan Boswell was staggering back from the Chequers in South Elmsall he thinks about midnight saw a man standing next to a white van he thinks maybe a Commer. He noticed that the man kept looking at his watch. So Alan nods to him and then staggers home. He said that he had never seen the van before. I have taken a statement his description is male white five foot ten or eleven maybe six foot quite well built wearing one of those roll neck jumpers fishermen have and dark trousers. He does admit that he had drunk 8 pints of Barnsley Bitter and a scotch." David handed him the statement. "I have given him the incident room telephone number if he remembers anything else."

4
The List

Thursday
14th April 1966

At 9am Renton arrived at the station, checked his tray in his office, there were a couple of files that needed to be looked at and then went to the prosecutor's office and found some leaflet's from the Attorney General's office about policing. At 10am he went to morning prayers, thankfully Walter Benson wasn't there so he brought the Chief and the others up to what was happening with the murder and about the post mortem report. He listened to what the others had to say and then the Chief excused him from the rest of the meeting. He went down to the collator's office for a much needed mug of black coffee. He sat down opposite Reg.

"So Ralph how is the party going for your engagement, have you fixed a date?"

"No not yet but there will be no official party, I have suggested we have it at the house but she has other ideas, both our parents have passed on. Jenny has two brothers living abroad the other lives in York. So I am stalling at the present but she has been dropping hints about Italy. So when this investigation is over and done with I will book the holiday and that will be that I hope but it would be nice to have a party for friends and colleagues at the house."

"Yes but can you put up with the constant reminders that you haven't done anything yet?"

"Enough of that how have you got on with list of Cooper's fellow soldiers?"

"I managed to find the right person to give me the list, he was loath to actually send me a list so I wrote it down and I have typed it up for you here you go." He handed it to Renton.

"Hmm 16 recruits 8 to Suez and 8 to Germany all from the north and one from further north Edinburgh, is that unusual I wonder?"

"The tiresome person at the other end of the line eventually explained that all the recruits are taken from several counties and all were born in 1934. Training started in autumn 1954."

"Righto a bit like the Pals Battalions in the first world war?"

"Yes don't mention it to Austin or he will go on for hours how the War Ministry were soooo wrong to do that."

"So going by the note that Cooper received one of these could be the killer. That would narrow it down to 15 rather than the male population of the world. So your next task is to find out where all these bods are now. See you at 4pm."

Renton then went back to the files in his office.

Reg was just about to start on the list when C/I Johnny Martin came in He made himself a coffee and put sixpence in the tin. He looked the list over and said "Reg this T Stewart on this list from Yorkshire you don't suppose it's our Terry Stewart thief and drunk. How old was this Stewart compared to our drunk."

"All the people on that list when it came out in 1954 were twenty years of age let me have a look through my card index."

The card index had thousands of cards indexed A to Z convicted and A to Z unconvicted and A to Z of persons who had been turned over but not arrested.
It also included females but that was a much smaller index. Both convicted and unconvicted had two files.

"Here we are Terence John Stewart born 1930 so now 35 years old 36 in June in the West Riding telephone there is only one T Stewart. On Terry's card it says next of kin is a sister Elsie Stewart."

Johnny said "He won't have a telephone, why would he, he hasn't got any friends I know of."

"So what is your interest in Terry then?"

Johnny said "I have just had an ear bending from Elsie saying Terry has been missing for over 2 weeks."

"Is that unusual then?"

"He only goes missing for a week and then usually returns gives Elsie a couple of quid, has his tea and then goes to the pub."

"So why did she single you out for this particular ear bashing?"

"We grew up next door to each other, but after the war I joined the police and moved into Doncaster and thought I had left her bloody family behind. Of course when her parents died she moved in with Terry to look after her precious brother. I think she is realising although she would never say it, her brother is an arsehole."

"So when did the A hole go missing."

"She says Friday 30th March. He works for the bookies, the Edwards brothers. She made him a flask of coffee and sandwiches which is usual. He then went off to a couple of race meetings with the brothers, but she doesn't know where certainly not Donny. She says he would have come back a week later about the 6th April."

"Okay I will mention it to the boss, we will have a debrief at 4pm today so come down then for that."

Debrief

By 4pm everyone was assembled in the murder room

Renton said "Who would like to go first?"

Steve said "Cooper was known in every pub from Armthorpe to Doncaster and beyond and had been thrown out of most at some stage his party trick was to get drunk then refuse to leave but most times when fronted up or he thought the police were coming he would leave quietly and onto the next pub. He was last seen Sunday dinnertime in the Wheatsheaf but left quietly. However he seemed quite flush with money, normally paying in change and not flashing five pound notes."

Renton nodded towards Jack

Jack said "Same thing he was well known but on the day before his death he was in South Elmsall in the Plough next to the market drinking with a Gerry Horton, they were deep in conversation but the beer was flowing and both were paying for beer and chasers in pound notes and not the usual change. Cooper left about 10pm in his cups. Horton then stayed talking to a woman and left with her at closing time and walked off towards the fire station, he apparently lives somewhere near."

"Which way did Cooper go do we know?"

"One of the regulars said he left the door open and he could see him sitting on a bench at the bus station, which is where people sit usually waiting for a taxi. When Horton left Cooper had disappeared. Maybe got a taxi or got one in Station Road."

"Righto, so here we have the reprobate Chief Inspector Johnny Martin who will relay the sad story of the disappearance of a T Stewart. The reason I am including this is because of the coincidence of the name on the list and we have someone of the same name. Over to you Johnny."

Johnny then relayed the conversation with Elsie.

Renton said "So we might have another, who knows, Reg is trying to track down the names on this list. So we need to find this Gerry Horton, because also on the list number 8 we have a G Horton from Yorkshire, all very strange just a coincidence, I think not .Can anyone here tell me about the Edwards brothers and what is Stewart's link to them.?"

Austin stood up "George and Francis Edwards, twins now in their sixties, but still sharp as tacks. George is the antique end and Francis always called Frank is the bookie although George helps out. Both born in Ireland family moved when the twins were toddlers, settled here in Doncaster.
They have a finger in a scrap metal and chop shop business. Both served in the West Yorkshire Regiment, both tough. Francis did a bit of bare knuckle boxing. He goes to various race meetings around the country and they travel to Ireland where they still have family and contacts. George also goes to Cologne every so often for the markets."

"Considering you are retired Austin how do you know all this current stuff?

Austin tapped his nose "Spies everywhere."

"Do you think they could have bumped off Stewart?"

"No he was useful to them he was a runner and errand boy. They wouldn't get involved in murder. They might rough someone up who crossed them but not murder."

"Right tomorrow Austin and I will go to see George and Frank do you know Francis?"

"We have met yes."

"Then you and Jack go and see him."

Austin said "Frank lives in a plush place near Tickhill and we will be going to Wetherby near the A1. You can drive Ralph."

"Of course sir." said Renton "At 6pm I shall be in the Red Lion and my wallet shall be open for exactly ten minutes. See you then."

6
The Edwards Brothers

Friday
15th April 1966

Before he left Renton said "Dennis your job today is to see your local contacts and see where Cooper and Stewart were before Cooper died. Not the pubs, but the cafe's and bookies see if they were in Doncaster."

Dennis headed for Dick's Diner.

4pm
Debrief
Frank said "Francis and his gang is that the right word perhaps I should say associates were at Cheltenham on 17th March, St. Patrick's Day. Arkle was the star of the day. Stewart was running errands as usual. Four days later they were at Aintree for the Grand National. The big winner was Team Spirit. Apparently Francis was well pleased with his winnings and treated his boys to several drinks. Francis then went to Wetherby to see George. For most of the week Stewart appeared on edge as if he was meeting waiting for someone or something to turn up. Francis paid them all off and as far as he knows Stewart went back to Doncaster. That was on a Wednesday. He was supposed to meet Francis and the others on the Monday to go to the races at York but he didn't show up. They think because he was flush he had a bit of stuff he was seeing."

Jack said "I spoke to Mick Connell who is ex job, only served 2 years and he is Francis Edward's chauffeur he said that usually Stewart turned up for these jobs with only change in his pocket, but this time he had a few bob and paid Francis £45 he owed him."

Renton said "Righto, well we saw George who started off a bit hostile but Austin smoothed him out talking about the old days in the trenches together. He knew Stewart had gone with Francis but when he didn't show up on the Monday he said Francis wasn't surprised. Austin asked him if he had heard anything about Cooper before and after death, Edwards said that Francis had said that he had been in his shop the Saturday before he died and was spreading a few quid around the races. He said we should see a Bunny Warren who had his finger on the Doncaster pulse." There was a ripple of laughter from the others.

"Righto so what have I said?" sad Renton.

Reg said "Victor William Warren you might know him from your past in the Intelligence Unit in the war."

"Really I don't recall anyone of that name I will make a few calls tonight. Steve, Tina what have you got?"

Tina said "Mrs Cooper didn't have a lot to say but she said that most times he would come in drunk and burble on about something he had happen to him, but if he was hiding something he would go straight to bed. But 2 weeks before he died he came in and said "The cook's come up trumps." She asked him what that meant, but he just went to bed. She said he did play cards occasionally with mates in South Elmsall probably with Gerry."

"Is Horton a cook?" said Renton.

There was no reply. Dennis put his hand up, Renton nodded to him.

"I did a few calls on some old friends. I found out that Cooper would go into Dick's Diner every Friday night, he stays open on a Friday until 8pm. Cooper would stoke up on food before he went out on the booze he went in the Friday before he died with a wallet full of cash. He normally paid in silver and coppers. Dick mentioned the money and Cooper said "Friends from the past paying their debt."

"Thank you Dennis so let me recap we have Cooper who is dead and Stewart who may be dead. Normally they don't have a pot to piss in and then suddenly they both have a lot of cash. So either they have been holding up a post office or they have found the end of the rainbow. Tomorrow we will have a briefing at 11am once Frank is back from prayers and sort out who will see this Bunny Warren chap. See you all tomorrow."

7
Stifado

Saturday
16th April 1966

Frank came down from morning prayers. He and Renton had decided not to tell the Chief about Stewart because after all he was only a missing person at this stage. Present was Austin Jack Reg Steve and Tina.

Frank said "The Chief has decided that from now on he will not attend weekend morning prayers and whoever the senior officer is, he shall contact him if there is an emergency."

"Righto, I contacted a pal from my time in the Intelligence corps and asked about Warren's past.
Apparently he was one of the intelligence officers for the fledgling SAS and the LRDG but was wounded and after recovering became their liaison officer. He is a very fluent speaker in several languages, French Arabic and Greek..His mother was Greek and because he spoke that language was used in Crete to do a bit of spying. Nearly got caught by the Gestapo, but managed to get back here then spent the rest of his war in Cairo. I just couldn't think where I knew him from and then remembered this Arab chap who circulated around the embassies in Cairo it was him. His codename was Lapin which is French for rabbit."
There was a ripple of laughter.

"I've known Bunny since he was a lad" said Austin. "His mum makes a mean stifado." There were blank looks from the others "Stifado is a Greek dish a sort of stew made from beef and onions and very warming for a cold bobby on a winter's night. Anyway Jack and I paid him a visit last night. He owns the barbers near the Diner, he and mum live above the barbers. His cousin Alex Warren ex commando, nasty bastard cuts the hair mind you I wouldn't let him cut mine. We showed Bunny the list we have of the National Service boys and a distant relative is Bernie Woods the last on the list he is now a shepherd in the middle of nowhere in Cumberland. Here is a telephone number of a post office. Woods calls it or pops in to see if there is any mail or calls for him his wife is Greek and a relative of Warren's mum.

"Excellent." said Renton "Reg could you call this number and set up a meeting with the good shepherd?"

Reg went across to his telephone made a couple of calls then returned to the briefing.

"The Post Office is at Penrith but Woods rings it from the back of beyond from a call box. He will ring them today at 1pm so I have asked them to ask him to go to Penrith Police Station on Monday for 1pm for an interview with you. I will delve into the police almanac find Penrith and set it up with them."

Just then Johnny Martin walked in.

"Hello murder team Ralph the Chief has just asked me to pop in and tell you he will be having a meeting with the newspapers on Monday here at 11am."

"Wonderful." said Renton "So all the lunatics will be lining up to confess. Frank you will have to be my representative at the meeting."

"Yes thank you for that."

Renton said to Johnny "Steve and I will be going to Penrith and you Johnny along with your officers can field the lunatics."

Renton said "So we are all off tomorrow except for Frank who is duty DI. Steve I will pick you up from home at 8.30am. For today sort out your paperwork and knock off at 2pm.

Reg went back to his desk found the police almanac then rang Penrith police station and set up the meeting he then rang Renton in his office and told him.

8
The Shepherd

Monday
18th April 1966

Renton picked up Steve and headed for the A1.
"Let's go the scenic route and head for Richmond, I know a nice little cafe where we can get a brew and then get to Penrith."

Arriving at Penrith just before 1pm they were shown into an office where there was an unhappy looking Chief Inspector

"I am Chief Inspector Lowther I understand that you are using my police station for an interview."

"Yes one of my officers spoke to an Inspector on Saturday and made the appointment for a basic witness statement being taken about something that may have happened in the past which may have been the cause of a vicious murder 5 days ago near Doncaster. I can ring my Chief and he will contact your Chief if it is a problem."

Renton reached for the telephone.

Very apologetically Lowther said "Oh there is no need for that I am sure. Your witness is in the canteen. I should warn you he smells strongly of sheep."

"Renton gave Lowther an evil grin and said "Well he would he is gainfully employed as a shepherd."

"Er yes umm yes follow me please."

Lowther introduce them to Bernie Woods and left

As Renton shook hands with Woods he introduced himself and Steve.

Woods said "Sorry about the smell I have just come from dipping the sheep."

"No problem." said Renton "Have you had anything to eat or a cuppa?"

"Yes thank you the canteen lady made me a bacon roll and a mug of tea."

Renton produced the list that Reg had written down he gave it to Woods. He then explained about Cooper being killed and Stewart being missing saying "Do you mind if my colleague makes a few notes and then take a statement."

"No not at all how can I help you."

"Can you help us with the names on here?"

Woods looked it over and said "This list is typical of the army the majority of the people went to Germany but one or two who were meant to be posted to Germany went to Suez instead".

Renton said "Cooper according to our pathologist was killed by a professional. Cooper was a drunk and as far as we can see he wasn't killed for money or anything like that so the only connection we can think of is something from his past. We had a series of murders in Doncaster 3 years ago and they were connected to the victims past. Do you remember all the people on this list?"

"Yes unforgettable some of them."

"So let's start with training where was that?"

"Catterick Camp a place not easy to forget probably the most miserable place on earth especially when it rains and believe me it does rain a lot."

"So let's talk about training and their personalities?"

"Well the 8 weeks was about getting everyone fit lots of physical training the instructor had been kicked out of the Gestapo for being too cruel. Drill also known as square bashing sometimes in double time. Able to hold a rifle and shoot it correctly and who would go where no square pegs in round holes. Also 2 going to Germany and 2 going to Suez would become lance jacks sorry corporals.No.1 Jimmy Campbell, very sporty, rugby mad and clever he was training to be a surveyor very likeable. Derek Carlyle would stir the pot then would step back. There were 4 shits, Cooper Stewart and Horton and their leader was Carlyle. Three groups emerged. Them and us which was Jimmy me and Fred Johnson and John Phillips and Ali Duggan and Bill Smith, Tommy Dawson, Dave Henson and Paul Rodgers all nice lads. The others kept out of it. If you want to know what happened in Germany you should talk to Fred he lives out there married a local girl. Also John Phillips stays in touch with some of the others"

"So how did they decide who would go where?"

"Well it was all about if you had any talents. The powers that be decided most of our group would be going to Germany. There was a lot of pressure because the troops in Germany were essentially guarding a perimeter that eventually would become the Berlin Wall."

"So who made the single stripe?"

"Alistair Duggan was made lance corporal and that really wound up Carlyle who was hoping to get it. Ali was a bit of a bookworm very quiet studying to be a chemist. At first he was hopeless, PT athletic football and cross country and drill. But he gradually improved. Carlyle and his cronies started picking on him and that's when we put a stop to it. Jimmy and Bill were both built like bulls and Carlyle and his bullies backed off. Horton was all muscle and no brains but Jim just laid him out with one punch. But what really got them was Ali turned out to be a crackshot. Six out of six bulls every time. Turned out his dad was an ex parachute regiment decorated with the MC and had taught him to shoot. So by the end of training Ali got the stripe.
They did promote Carlyle later but that happened in Germany."

"So who should we talk to about Germany?"

"Fred or JP in Leeds. I will give you their telephone numbers."

"Righto Steve here will just write out a statement about what you have said, read through it and then sign if you are happy with it. I should warn you that you may have to go to court when we get the killer."

Steve wrote the statement and Woods signed it.

Renton said "Now for the thousand dollar question if you could pick one person from the list capable of killing Cooper who would it be?"

"Carlyle without a doubt he was a nasty piece of work."

"You said Cooper was in Carlyle's gang so why would he kill a friend?"

"He would have slit his granny's throat if he had to."

Renton said "If you think of anything please call me on this number?" Renton handed him a small card. "Can we give you a lift anywhere?"

"No the wife is picking me up do you know that Ali died in Germany in some sort of shooting accident."

"Do you have any information on that?"

"No the army are very good at covering up anything detrimental to them but ask Fred Woods I bet he knows what's what."

"Really then we need to talk to the others, thank you."

They shook hands and left.

Sitting in the car Renton said "Now that paints a different picture for me Duggan dying in Germany we need to get a hold of Johnson and Phillips."

9
Berlin Again

Tuesday
19th April 1966

Everyone was in the murder room mugs in hand.

"Frank how did the Chief get on with the newspapers?" said Renton

"It was good, the Chief handled it well. One reporter said that he had information that there was a body on the butter cross gushing blood. The Chief said where did you get the information about that then the reporter said my sources are confidential the Chief said I would hope that you reporters would work with us the reporter was very quiet after that. Henry Sykes was there. He told me later that the reporter is an Alfie Wormald about 19 out to make a name for himself."

"Does he work for the Post?"

"No I think he is a freelance and then sells his story to whoever is willing to pay."

"Righto, Steve please relate to our congregation what the good shepherd had to say."

Steve then read out the statement about the conversation.

Renton said "So the sting in the tail was at the end when he said about Duggan dying in Germany. So was it to do with Carlyle and his gang. You could hear the distaste in his voice when he mentioned Carlyle. I think the crux could be about his death. So Steve you can contact Johnson in Germany and Dennis ring Phillips and make an appointment for me to see him Reg can you see if you can find out anything about Duggan's death. Jack and Austin see if you can prise something out of Bunny about Duggan Steve and Tina can you go and see Elsie Stewart have a look through Stewart's possessions see if there is anything from his past. See you all back here at 4pm."

Renton said to Frank "Can you fix up to meet Sergeant Smith the Elmsall sergeant?"

Frank went into the collators office and picked up the telephone. He came back a few minutes later.

"He will be here in the collators at 12.30."

Right on 12.30 Sergeant Smith walked into the collators, he shook hands with Reg who said "Long time Smudge?"

"Aye that it is."

As Frank introduced Renton to the sergeant, he realised just how tall the sergeant was at least six foot six inches and with what could only be described as a wild moustache. They shook hands.

"You know Reg then sergeant?" Renton said.

"I do that we have known each other a good few years, please call me Smudge everyone does. I started here in Donny after the war and then became the beat bobby in Bentley, then got my stripes and the old Chief wanted me to look after the thin blue line in the coal triangle."

(He pronounced coal as coil)

"So you are well informed on what is going on in your particular patch?"

"Aye right enough. Most of the lads served in the war so we have a close bond and a few extra ears on the ground."

"So you know about Eric Cooper and maybe Terence Stewart."

"Aye, I know about Cooper and the butter cross and Frank mentioned Stewart being missing, he is many things but from what I know about him he always turns up back to his sister when he needs grub. They meet in the Plough near the market in Elmsall mind you they frequented every pub from there to Barnsley, along with Gerry Horton. They also had a card school in the Market inspector's cabin usually Thursday night I am told and having not seen Stewart's ugly mug of late I reckon summat has happened to him."

"You are told?"

"Aye I have a spy in their card school a lot of what they are involved in gets talked at their card nights."

"What can you tell us about Cooper and Stewart?"

"Cooper has a reputation in the boozers, he is full of gob and likes to make a song and dance when they kick him out. Stewart all mouth and trousers I allus thought he was a bit of a jessie. Horton all muscle and no brains good looking lad has a way with the ladies the problem is he prefers the married ones."

Renton then told him about how Cooper was killed.

"Well if it is a professional then once Stewart turns up the same way that's the link. From what Frank says it could happen to anyone connected to their past, so not an indiscriminate killing as some might think" he handed a piece of paper to Frank "Hartwell's statement."

"Well thanks for coming Smudge and let us know if you get anything more."

"Surely, see you sometime Reg."

When he had left Renton said "Big chap."

"Yes ex Guards not a lot gets past him and his lads."

4pm debrief

Steve said "I contacted Mrs Johnston in Germany, her husband Fred is in Whitby seeing his mum and Dad. So I contacted him there, he is coming in here on Thursday, be here at 1pm."

Dennis said "John Phillips has a newsagents in Leeds Phillips and Son. He is half day closing tomorrow and can see you from 12.30 onwards the next time would be Sunday. So I made an appointment to see him tomorrow at 1pm."

"Excellent." said Renton "So a busy two days for me and you Steve, I will pick you up tomorrow at yours at 10am.Reg what have you got for us?"

"No luck with the army, so I rang my contact from the Poppy Killings. He is going to ring me back later or tomorrow with what he knows."

"Jack what about you and Austin?"

"Bunny was a bit reluctant so he made a couple of phone calls." said Jack "He said that apparently Duggan's rifle or gun jammed and the breech exploded and caught him in the face killing him."

"Tina what about you and Elsie?"

"I took Dennis along with me. She is living hand to mouth, very spartan and clean inside but Terry's bedroom you wipe your feet when you leave, looks like a bomb has gone off. We gave it a thorough search. Elsie never went in because he would go loopy if she tried to clear it up. Inside the wardrobe was an old jacket and inside was this."
She produced what looked like a very old leather document case."Just look inside." she said.

Austin said "That is an officers despatch bag used in the first war for messages to be conveyed by runners or cyclists from officer to officer, from HQ to the trenches."

Renton opened it and pulled out an envelope and a wad of fivers and one pound notes. Frank counted the money.

"One hundred pounds." he said.

Renton opened the letter and read the note it said "Terry old mate, I'm seeing Eric and then you and maybe Gerry, see you soon". It was signed Dekko.

Renton said "So the plot thickens. Tina can you take all this to Peter and see if he can get any prints off it. If they find anything we will have keep it for evidence, otherwise I think it should be returned to Elsie. I will endorse your pocket book to that effect. We will keep the wallet and the note. Shall we call it a day."

10
John Phillips

Wednesday
20th April 1966

Renton collected Steve from his house and they set off for Leeds. They stopped in Hunslet on the way and found a bakers and enjoyed a bacon roll and a cuppa. They then continued on their way arriving at the newsagents at 1pm. Renton introduced himself and Steve.

John Phillips answered the door and said "Good timing I've just put the kettle on."
He led them up the stairs and directed them to the dining room end of the flat. He then brought out a coffee pot cups cream sugar and some slices of fruit cake.

"Do you live here alone John?"

"No my wife Peggy is in Wakefield today looking after her dad he had a fall recently. I am led to believe that you want to talk about the chaps who served with me in the National Service."

"Yes that is correct do you mind if my colleague makes notes, we may have to ask you to give a statement."

"Yes and yes."

Do you remember Eric Cooper and Terence Stewart?"

"Oh yes how could I forget a right pair of things along with Gerry Horton and Carlyle. Without them the training and service would have been a pleasure."

"Which one used the nickname Dekko?"

"Bloody Derek Carlyle the leader of that little gang of cretins."

"Can you tell me about Alistair Duggan in training and his death?"

"Such a shame Ali was a clever lad studying to be a chemist but his real ambition was to be a doctor bit of a bookworm, quiet lad. But Carlyle and his cronies singled him out for a bit of ribbing and bullying. Some of us got together and included him in our group. Country boy from Lincolnshire can you believe he was 20 and had never been drunk. The basic training was about getting you fit and ironing out any weaknesses. To start with he was hopeless at athletics and PT and couldn't march arms and legs all over the place" he laughed "but we helped him along Horton was all muscle and no common sense and took delight in tripping him up that sort of thing, by the fourth week he was getting into his stride but Horton persisted in being a pain in the backside and knocked him down one evening during a shining parade. Big mistake Jimmy Campbell intervened and Horton challenged him. Jimmy laid him out with a single punch, it was beautiful. From the fifth week we started doing rifle firing on the range and you should have seen Ali he was a crackshot, 6 bulls out of 6 every time. In the last week there were various tests and we knew that of those being posted to Germany one would get his single stripe. Ali by this time was well ahead in the stakes for that single stripe he pipped Carlyle to the stripe. Carlyle was not happy. I got the other stripe because I was going to Suez. But at the last minute I went to Germany. Tommy Dawson got the other because he ended up going to Suez."

"What can you tell us about Alistair's death in Germany?"

"Not a lot really, the army are very good at hushing things up. Fred Johnson might be able to help because his wife was a nurse, she is German and was at the military hospital they took Ali to he died I think either on the way or in the hospital. Apparently he was unconscious until he died. His rifle had some sort of a back fire as he tried to clear it. I always thought it was a bit dodgy because he was quite expert with the rifle and he kept it spotlessly clean unless of course someone got to it before him."

"Where were the rifles kept?"

"At the end of the barrack room and were in a rack locked up the lance corporal on duty had the key. There was the usual rumours was it suicide, murder or an accident."

"What do you think?"

"At the time I was out on the perimeter doing guard duty and it happened in the late afternoon they would be cleaning their kit ready to relieve us at 10pm.It wasn't suicide he had so much to live for. He did have a few problems in Germany and you should ask Fred he became a bit of a detective trying to find out the truth for Ali's dad."

Renton showed John the list he had of them all prior to training.

He then said "Eric Cooper has been murdered near Doncaster and it is up to me and my team to find the killer. Looking at this list who do you think had the necessary to kill Cooper. Our pathologist said that the killer was a professional and had probably killed before?"
"The only one with a bit of acumen and evil enough to murder would have to be Carlyle."

Renton said "But wasn't Cooper one of his little gang along with Stewart and Horton."

"Yes he was but when Carlyle wanted something he went for it there was a rumour in barracks that he had something going outside in Berlin and he was always flush with money. Our army pay wasn't exactly startling. He had worked in a slaughterhouse and was quite a cold character. He was very good at lighting the blue touch paper and standing back if you know what I mean."

"What about Campbell can you tell us about him?"

Big chap, rugby mad training to be a surveyor, apparently his dad had connections at the mines in South Africa. Last I heard he was over there."

"Bill Smith?"

"Yes apprentice blacksmith bit of a boxer. One of the PT instructor's liked to show off in the ring he took Bill on 3 rounds later he was on his knees. He said when Bill hit him it was like being hit by an express train. Bill was posted to Suez in my place. He is now a blacksmith somewhere something to do with horse racing."

"Righto, Steve here will take a statement about what you saw in basic training and what went on. We are seeing Fred Johnston tomorrow."

"Oh he is here in England. Can you give him my regards and ask him to visit if he has the chance."

"Yes, of course thank you for the drinks and cake. Here is my card if you think of anything else then give me a call. Oh by the way what did you think of Stewart?"

"Idiot did what he was told by Carlyle and Horton liked his drink more than once he had to sober up sharpish for guard duty."

Later in the car Steve said "So any thoughts about the killer."

"The more I hear about Carlyle the more I think he is our man, but you never know always keep an open mind."

They made good time and got back to the station in time for 4pm.

Steve then read out the statement he had taken from John Phillips.

Jack said "Sounds like Carlyle could be the killer, I wonder or maybe Horton?"

Renton said "Well we will need a bit more proof that's for sure Tina how did you get on with Elsie?"

"We told her about the missing persons report and she thanked us for the cash Peter couldn't find anything on the cash letter or the pouch."

Frank said "I got a call from the Chief earlier on he has applied to the Attorney General to get the official Army report on Duggan's death he was told they would see what they could do but could be a problem it being a military affair."

"If Carlyle was capable of setting up Duggan then perhaps he is capable of killing his old comrades but why is what we have to find out. Fred Johnson coming in tomorrow so might find a little piece of the jigsaw."

11
Sandall Beat Wood

Thursday
21st April 1966

Renton had just finished shaving and put on his shirt and could smell Jenny frying his favourite breakfast, kippers. The telephone rang in the hall he heard Jenny answer it.

She said "It's for you Ted."

"Yes Ted what have you got?" said Renton

"Morning boss Terry Stewart has been found dead as a doornail same M.O as Cooper in Sandall Beat Wood. Dennis is on his way to get you."

"Sandall Beat Wood is that in Doncaster?

"Oh yes."

"Thanks Ted." he went into the kitchen and finding a kipper cut up he stuffed a bit in his mouth and took a swig of his coffee. He managed to finish the kipper just as there was a beep outside. Jenny gave him his tie ready to put on.

He said "That is a very neat knot."

Jenny handed him his jacket and said "With three brothers who couldn't tie a knot for toffee it was down to me to make sure they were ready for school and later college."

He got in the car and looked at his wristwatch 7.25am.

"Okay Dennis tell me about Sandall Beat Wood and what have we got.?"

"Some say Sandall Beat Wood was originally part of the mighty Sherwood Forest its near the A630.In Victorian times it was landscaped for the peasants to see a bit of greenery away from the slums they lived in whilst the Gentry rolled past in their horse and carriages. They couldn't tax fresh air.

"Bit cynical."

"It is a nice place to come, bring the kids kick a ball walk the dog have a picnic. There are parts of the wood that are dark but there is a wide path we can drive on originally it's where the nobs drove their pony and traps."

Just then they arrived at the wood and Renton saw how dark it had become but mainly on their right whereas on the left it seemed more open. On the darker side Renton could see something like a hut or shack.

"Dennis what's that over there?"he pointed to the shack.

"It was originally a woodsmen's hut used years ago for when they managed the forest and coppiced the trees. But after the war the council took it over then about 5 years ago it was locked up and forgotten about. I used to bring my kids here and say it was where the Bogey man lived."

They arrived at the scene but parked twenty feet away from the body near Peter's car. A uniformed bobby was there with his dog and Peter Johns was there taking photographs.

Dennis said "Boss this PC Jed Norman he found the body."

Jed saluted him

Renton shook his hand "What time did you find him?" Renton could see that Stewart was in a sitting position tied to a tree his head almost hanging off.

"It was five to six I was taking the dog for his last walk at the end of our night shift, Danko the dog sniffed him out. I thought checking for a pulse was a waste of time but as you can see he is definitely dead. Bit strange though not a lot of blood here."

Just then Doctor Wells arrived.

"What ho chaps hmm yes definitely dead, but not a lot of blood obviously killed somewhere else I would say."

Renton said "Why has he been tied to the tree then Doc?"

"Like the other one making a statement I would say look how close he is to the path, the killer wants him to be seen."

The mortuary men arrived and took out the familiar wooden box.

Doctor Wells said to Peter "Have you finished here Peter then my men can take the body away before the public appear?"

"Yes Doctor thank you."

"I will start the pm at 11am Ralph I think we can safely say he was garrotted the same way, anything untoward then I will ring Reg cheerio for now."

Renton said "Pc Norman do you walk your dog round the wood regularly when on nights?"

"Yes sir in fact I bring him at the end of most shifts unless we are on a call."

"Have you ever seen a vehicle anywhere near that shack before?"

"No sir."

"Righto then you had better go home and get some shuteye."

"Yes sir." he saluted and left.

As Renton and Peter went back to their vehicles Renton said "I take it you took some photographs of the tyre tracks on the other side of the path opposite to the body?"

"Yes sir, I think they will show that the vehicle was either pointing towards the body or had reversed up to it."

Once Peter and PC Norman had left Renton said to Dennis "Can you drive up to that shack, I will walk to it see you there."

Dennis parked away from the shack and Renton walked up to him.

"Do you still carry a key" in the boot and some evidence bags."
(Key was slang for a jemmy).

Renton took out a torch and looked at the path up to the shack, he could see what looked like tyre tracks on the ground up to the door.

"Dennis get on the radio and get Peter Johns back here."

When Dennis had radioed up Peter returned to them.

"When did you say the council locked this up for good?"

"Five years ago."
"Look at that padlock, I would say it is brand new and certainly not been in use for the last 5 years. You two can look away if you wish."

Renton then used the jemmy to force the padlock, he put on his gloves and put the padlock in a bag. He opened the two doors and went in the shack using the torch, he found the light switch but nothing happened. Renton said "Peter do you have a torch?"

Peter came in and passed him a torch.

He looked around the shack and in the corner found a mattress he shone the light on it. It was soaked in blood. "Peter can you photograph all this while I hold the torch for you."

Renton waited until Peter had finished then using a stick he lifted the mattress underneath was a blanket also soaked in blood and some rope. Peter photographed them. Renton placed them inside separate bags. He then rolled up the thin mattress and put that in a bag.

"Righto chaps let us depart. Peter in this other bag is a padlock can you see if you can find a fingerprint, it could be the print of the killer. Take a smear of blood from the mattress and then can you take the rope and blanket for the Doc to test the blood against our victims."

Before they left Dennis tied up the door with some rope from the car.

12
Post Mortem

Thursday
21st April 1966

Renton went into the murder room it was 9am. Everyone was making a drink so once they had settled down he said "Shortly I will be seeing the Chief to update him on the events from this morning. Early this morning PC Jed Norman a Police dog handler was nearing the end of his night shift and was giving his dog a last walk before he went home. He was in Sandall Beat Wood it was five minutes to six when his dog which was ahead of him started barking. He ran up to the dog and found Terence Stewart tied to a tree in a sitting position with his throat in the same condition as Coopers. There was a lack of blood on the ground so he had been killed somewhere else. Doctor Wells arrived and pronounced death. He didn't say when. After Peter had taken photographs the body was taken away. There were tyre tracks on the other side of the path opposite the body and those tyre tracks led me to a shack in a darker part of the wood about three hundred yards from the body. In the shack we found a mattress, blanket and ropes soaked in blood. So presumably the killer kept Stewart in the shack maybe killed him there then transported the body to where he was found by the dogman."

Frank said "Does the blood belong to Stewart?"

Renton said "Doc Wells will be testing the blanket and ropes very soon. But first I would like Tina and Jack to go and see Elsie and break the news. Also Steve it's about time you attended a post mortem which will start at 11am, but be back for 1pm because we have Fred Johnson coming in. Righto I am going to see the Chief."

Tina and Jack went to see Elsie.

Frank said to Dennis "Take me to this hut so I can have a butchers."

They arrived to find Peter sitting in his van sorting out his paperwork

Frank said "So have you got anything Peter?"

"The tyre tracks here are identical to those near the path where Stewart was."

Renton "How can you be so sure?"

Peter said "The front offside tyre is almost bald from the outside to the centre of the tread."

Frank said "So our killer has a vehicle, he takes Stewart to this shack keeps him in here kills him and then ties the body to a tree next to a well used path down the slope over there. The big question is why does he keep him here for a few days and then kill him why not kill straight away like Cooper."

Peter packed away his light and cameras and they all went back to the station.

Renton came back into the room Reg said to him "Can you telephone the doc he has already started on the post mortem so you are off the hook Steve."

Renton rang the mortuary.

"Ah yes Ralph when I looked at the body in the wood I noticed the bruising on his wrists and ankles so I couldn't wait so after some breakfast I started the post mortem. I think he was tortured over a period of time. There is skin tissue on the ropes from his wrists and ankles. Also bruising on his face I think he was beaten up to the point of unconscious then revived and then when he was awake beaten again. Obviously to make him talk about whatever the killer wanted to know. Also not a lot in his stomach so he was deprived of food maybe just water to keep him on the edge so to speak. I think he was killed last night so I would say about 8 hours before the dog found him 10pm to midnight that's about as close as I can get. Because of the lack of blood at the scene he was probably dumped maybe a couple of hours before he was found. Oh and he got the double wire treatment."

Renton put the receiver down and then made a coffee.

Tina and Jack came in.

"How did it go?" Renton said.

Tina said "Very tearful, she said he was always mixing with the worst sorts, we didn't tell her otherwise."

"Righto, Can I remind you all to make up your pocket books as soon as you can, Steve let me know when Fred Johnson arrives."

13
Fred Johnson

Thursday
21st April 1966

Steve showed Fred Johnson into the new witness interview room adjacent to the front office but away from the public's view and asked the front office PC to ring Renton. Renton arrived and introduced himself and they shook hands.

"Do you mind if I call you Fred and for my colleague to make notes?"

"Yes fine."

"It's very good of you to see us while you are on your holidays."

"I came over to see mum and dad, mum is not too well at the moment they are now retired to Whitby and I am on my way to see John in Leeds before I drive back to Cologne. I was intrigued as to why you want to see me. I understand it is to do with my time in the National Service."

"On 13th April Eric Cooper was found dead and this morning Terence Stewart was also found dead, both had been murdered possibly by the same person. Obviously I cannot tell you how. You were in training with them during National Service."

"I saw about Cooper in the Post, it said his throat had been slashed."

"You don't seem very surprised by their deaths?"

"They ran with a rough crowd in Germany, neither of them were pleasant people."

"We have spoken to John Phillips and Bernie Woods, both said they had a formed a gang of sorts."

"Yes I take it you may have served in the army and chaps stick together but those two along with Gerry Horton were led by a Derek Carlyle who was very manipulative and he used them to pick on others especially during our basic training."

"Can you tell us about Alistair Duggan?"

"Nice chap clever, studying to be a chemist but ultimately wanted to be a doctor. The gang started on him during training but a group of us kept them at bay. At the end of training 2 people are promoted to Lance Corporal one going to Germany and one to Suez. Carlyle was angling for the stripe but they gave it to Alistair. Carlyle was furious he thought he should have got it. He did get a stripe but in Germany after he and his "boys" fitted up Alistair who was demoted."

"Can you help us with the mystery surrounding Alistair's death?"

"According to the army report he was cleaning a rifle but actually he was clearing the rifle when it back fired or exploded in his face he died shortly after. Those in the barrack room at the time were questioned by the Military Police."

"We are told that Duggan was quite skilled with firearms so how could his rifle have jammed."

"Because it wasn't his it was thicky Hortons. I think it was a set up by Carlyle to injure or kill Duggan. There was a lot of bad blood between them. By this time Alistair had been demoted and should have been out on the perimeter with his squad but Carlyle had been promoted in his place and was conveniently out of the way on the perimeter guard. The squad always cleaned and checked their weapons in pairs before they went out to do the guard. Because Horton was such a plank he was paired up with Alistair who was not only the best shot but also adept with weapons unlike Horton. Alistair and the others would have taken over from Carlyle's squad. The other corporal was John Phillips."

"Did you ever get to see the Army report on his death?"

"Not a chance, you might be able to get it through official channels because you now have these murders to investigate but it will be swallowed up in reams of paperwork."

"You said Alistair was demoted why was that?"

"A group of the squad went out for a booze up and they roped Alistair into it. They went to a club in Berlin the Blue Iguana. Alistair had never been drunk but I reckon they spiked his drinks and he was posted absent without leave because he didn't appear for the muster parade the next morning. You could see his bed was made up and had not been slept in. I think they locked him up in a room in the club. His memory of it was very foggy. So he gets back to barracks and is placed on a charge by the adjutant and hauled up in front of the CO and demoted and given a couple of weeks fatigues in the cookhouse. They gave his stripe to Carlyle and one to Cooper who then was in charge of the orderly room, all the mail and various orders in and out."

"Do you know anything about Duggan's family?"

"His dad has a farm somewhere in Lincolnshire. After National Service he contacted me and asked if I could help him to re-open the inquiry. He knew I had stayed in Germany so perhaps thought I could get to the bottom of it. He got nowhere with the Army."

Renton then put the list of recruits in front of Fred and pointed to Campbell.

"Can you tell me about him?"

"Jimmy Campbell, big bugger, rugby mad, fit as a butchers dog knocked around with Tommy Dawson another rugby nut. Jimmy mentioned at the time he was thinking of joining the regulars. He was a good shot and handled all the army stuff easily. He would have gone through the ranks that's for sure. He was halfway through a chartered surveyor's course. But he did get bored easily especially with paperwork more of an action type really."

"Fred looking at this list who do you reckon could be our killer?"

"Carlyle."

"Is that because you don't like him?"

"My degree is in psychology but I teach maths so going on personalities and character I could say Horton but as they say broad in the shoulder thick in the head. But Carlyle had brains and a sort of animal cunning."

"Do you know what happened to Carlyle after National Service?"

"He was very pally with someone in that club, the Blue Iguana club. Ali did say that Carlyle and his gang spent a lot of off duty time there. Rumour was that the club was owned by some ex Nazi but I think that was just the gossips stirring the pot. Carlyle was promoted to acting sergeant in the Motor Transport section and responsible for chauffeuring the brass around. He may have stayed on doing that. After we had done the two years I was in Berlin with my soon to be wife in a restaurant and Carlyle came in with a couple of American officer types, all dressed in suits."

Renton said "Steve here will take a short statement from you and here is my card, if you think of anything else then don't hesitate to call me. If you are back in Cologne and you need to tell me something you can always reverse the charge. I will check with our admin person but I am sure it will be fine."

Steve took the statement then showed Fred back to his car.

Renton and Steve went down to the collators Reg was on the telephone, he put the receiver down and said "Positive match between the blood on the mattress, blanket and the rope for Stewart

14
Debriefing

4pm

Renton waited for everyone to settle down with a drink also there was PC Norman.

"Doctor Wells said that Stewart was tied up with the rope wrists and ankles. His blood matches the blood on the mattress and blanket. He was the beaten until unconscious and revived and then beaten up and revived. He wasn't given any food and only water. We had Fred Johnson in today. The rifle that killed Duggan was being cleared not cleaned by Duggan and it belonged to Horton."

"Set up." said Jack

"Yes that's what Fred thought. Steve made notes and they are here for you all to read. Reg and Austin we need to find out where Duggans dad lives. He served with the Paras in the war and won the MC."

Tina put her hand up. Renton nodded.

"Elsie came in and she said she wants to see Terry, so I said I would say when and where."

Peter came in."Here are the photographs of Stewart. I found that the tyre tracks at the shack match those at the tree where Stewart was so the killer has a vehicle. Also I have found a partial print from the padlock. It looks like it could be a thumb print. I have sent the print to Ted's mate at the fingerprint bureau at the Yard."

"Excellent any questions?"

Frank said "One thing bugging me is that Cooper and Stewart our resident drunks who never had a pot to piss in, had a lot of cash in their possession before they died so why and where from?"

"Yes good point Frank. So Steve and Tina bookies, money lenders ask around tomorrow Jack and Dennis same thing for you but anywhere between Doncaster towards South Elmsall."

The telephone in the collators rang. Reg answered it then walked back and said "Chief's secretary boss can you be in morning prayers tomorrow Henry Sykes will be there but with Doubting Thomas"

"Oh God I need a pint, 6pm the wallet will be open for 10 minutes. Briefing tomorrow 11am after prayers."

15
The Duggan Family

Friday
22nd April 1966

Renton arrived at the station at 9.00am ,checked his tray and then went into the collator's and made a cup of coffee. Having finished it he straightened his tie to leave for morning prayers. As he left Reg said "Walter is waiting for you."

Renton knocked on the Chief's door bang on 10am and entered. With the Chief was, Chief Inspector Fox, Inspector Hornby, Sergeant Ramsden, DCI Johnny Martin a new face and Walter Benson.

Before Benson could say something the Chief said "I would like to welcome newly promoted Tim Waters who is with us for a month he is from the Met and doing a project on the County forces for the Home Office. He has something to say which we all have been thinking about Tim over to you."

"Good morning everyone, it's about what the Police Act of 1964 will achieve in four years. On the 1st October 1968 Doncaster will amalgamate with Barnsley, Dewsbury, Halifax, Huddersfield and Wakefield and will be called the West Yorkshire Police. This will be happening throughout the country. I should also tell you that means that instead of 117 constabulary's there will be 49 Police Forces in England and Wales."

Inspector Hornby said "I have heard a rumour that the Watch Committees will be replaced with a Police Authority and ultimately they will be governed by the Home Office."

Inspector Waters said "There are plans to change the idea of the Watch Committee because each force will be bigger than a constabulary and obviously cost more."

The Chief said "I would like Ralph to give us the latest on the two murders and where the investigation is at. But first I would like to say that the release to the newspapers so far has been a complete waste of time. They will only print sensationalism such as "man found with his throat slashed gushing blood. I didn't say that I wonder where they got that from." The Chief flashed a look at Benson. He continued "Lunatic confessions such as it is a warning that aliens will be taking over Yorkshire. There will be no press release about Stewart's murder."

Benson was about to say something. The Chief put his hand up "Let Ralph speak questions later."

Renton then explained where Stewart was found and what he and Dennis had found inside the shack and his conversation with Fred Johnson.

Benson said "So we have a deranged killer on the loose again then."

Renton said "No we have a man who targeted two men and killed them in a very professional way. We believe that something that happened eleven years ago has influenced the killings. There is no danger to the public at large." He emphasized the words eleven and no.

Benson was about to say something else but the Chief said "Enough we have other items on the agenda like disturbances at certain pits in the coal triangle. Thank you Ralph get back to your team."

Renton left and went down to the collators to find Frank making a mug of tea.

"Did you enjoy prayers?"

"Does Benson come to prayers when you are there Frank?"

"No he saves himself for you. Did you know that the Chief is thinking of having a traffic light system installed by Jock the carpenter outside his door because Benson never knocks and just barges in so when the green light shows the door unlocks.

"He really doesn't like Benson."

"Who does? But why is he still coming if he is retired. Was Henry Sykes there?"

"Yes. There was an inspector from the Met allegedly but he must be from the Home Office a Tim Waters, he spoke about the amalgamation of Doncaster with five others and becoming the West Yorkshire Police. The best bit was Bill Hornby mentioned about the scrapping of the Watch Committee you should have seen Benson's face."

The telephone rang Reg answered it "For you." He gave it to Renton who said "Yes of course."

"Henry Sykes is coming down for a chat."

He came into the incident room and Renton said "Coffee?"

Henry said "Yes thank you no milk and no sugar."

They sat down and Henry said "I never really realised just how obnoxious Walter could be and seems to like goading you and the Chief. So to that end he will be formally retired and told not to interfere in police matters. It's obvious he has been speaking to the press and in particular a young reporter called Alfie Wormald do you know of him?"

Renton said "I have heard that name before I will see if any of the others have spoken to him."

Henry said "I have spoken privately to the Chief and we think disbanding the Watch Committee and having a committee made up of councillors and magistrates is the way forward."

Renton thanked Henry and showed him back to the front office.

As he waited for the rest of the team to arrive he said to Reg "Have you ever been on holiday then Reg."

"No we don't go away Mrs Prestleigh loves her house and the garden. The front garden is full of white roses and all things pretty. Our back garden is huge so it is full of vegetables, herbs and more pretties. We also have a large patio at the back door with something I am told is called a gazebo. Mrs Prestleigh has been a member of the WI from birth it seems she is the treasurer for them which means that they always have their committee meetings more often at our house come rain or shine. That's why I am always here. You were married once."

"I know what you mean."

Gradually everyone arrived in time for the briefing.

Jack said "I've just seen Ted he said the Chief put Kipper firmly in his place."

"Yes thank God or he would still be banging on about the killer he did allude to our previous killer."

"Once everyone was in place Renton said "Austin what have you got?"

"I went to the Legion last night and saw Wingco Harvey. Alistair Duggan senior born in 1918 in Lincoln dad was a farmer. So sixteen years old gets his girlfriend Alice pregnant her dad not a man to be trifled with insists they marry which they do. She moves into the farm gives birth to a boy they call him Alistair.1938 second son arrives Alexander. Something about the letter A grandad is Andrew.1939 Alistair now 20 enlists in the army ends up at Dunkirk. Comes home, eventually as the Parachute Regiment is formed he volunteers. By 1944 he is a company sergeant major and is involved in the D-Day Campaign. Lieutenant Colonel is badly wounded so Duggan under fire wipes out a machine gun nest picks up said Colonel and on his way back also get seriously wounded. But they both get back safely. Duggan then spends rest of the war in hospital and then gets a wheelchair he also gets the Military Cross. Former colonel is extremely well off and landed Gentry gives Duggan a lump sum and a pension for life. Duggan ploughs the money into the farm. Duggan junior dies in 1955 followed by mum Alice."

"Who is Wingco Harvey?"said Renton

"He was the pilot who dropped Duggan and his men into France in 1944 and is now an unofficial historian of all things D-Day."

"Steve any luck with Campbell?"

"Nothing I think Reg should contact his army pal."

Just then the collator's telephone rang. Reg answered it, wrote something down on his pad and then handed Renton a note.

"Bernie Woods can you ring him on this number?"

Renton looked at the number and then said "Jack Tina and Dennis Sandall Wood for you. Talk to the dog walkers anybody there see if they have seen any activity near the hut. Reg get on and see if you can find out anything about Campbell and Tommy Dawson he apparently worked at Carlisle Station we need to track them down everyone back at 4pm."

16
Brampton

Friday
22nd April 1966

Renton went to his office and rang the number on the piece of paper he identified himself.

Bernie Woods said "After I got home the wife said what about that diary you kept when you were in Germany. I had completely forgotten about it. So I had a look in the loft and found it amongst my stuff from the fifties. The diary was a sort of memory. In September 1955 I wrote "Cannot believe it about Ali, he was so switched on about weapons. He said before he died that he wrote to his mum and dad every week and had sent him a really important letter about what was happening out there in Germany."

"We really need to find dad and what that letter is about" said Renton."Do you know where dad is living?"

"He said they lived near Brampton and he was from Lincolshire. He said when he was a kid he and his mates would go to Torksey looking for Viking treasure."

"Did you know that the rifle that exploded actually belonged to Horton?" said Renton.

"Well well that is interesting. There is another reference here to the Blue Iguana Club in Berlin, that's where they got Ali drunk."

"What sort of club drinking music or strippers?"

"All of those things full of degenerates some sort of brothel I think. Also in here is the name of Henry Kowalski he was the senior cook. Part of Ali's punishment was washing up hundreds of pans and peeling spuds all part of the army's way of keeping you in line they call it discipline. Ali said that Carlyle seemed to be very pally with this Kowalski and remembers seeing them together in Berlin. He found out that this cook could speak German and Polish. The cook had a sort of small office and in the afternoons was always on the telephone."

"Just between you me and the gatepost Stewart was found dead yesterday in the same fashion as Cooper. Any thoughts?"

"Carlyle covering his tracks from the past I think."

"Well thanks for that if you think of anything more give me a call."

Renton returned to Reg "Do you have a road map of England?"

"But of course, Bartholomew's Cycle maps."

"What about Lincolnshire Brampton or Torksey."

"Torksey Lock quite famous in medieval times."

"Why?"

The Vikings sailed down the Humber into the Trent and then raped and pillaged Scunthorpe and Newark. The name Thorpe comes from a Viking word. Here is Torksey and let me see. Ah yes here is Brampton the flat countryside of Lincolnshire."

"I cannot imagine Mrs Prestleigh on a bicycle made for two."

Oh no not her it was my first love Daphne Inglesby cycling and camping very good for getting close to the girls. So cosy when it rains, so chilly and they need a cuddle just to keep them warm of course, Brampton north of Torksey about 10 miles. I will contact Lincoln Police and see if they know the farm but if not a word with the Farmers Union should do it."

"Briefing at 4pm see you then."

4pm

Renton told the team about his conversation with Bernie Woods." So we now have a Henry Kowalski to add to the list and the Blue Iguana Club Reg?"

"Duggan's farm is near Brampton. He has a very good reputation amongst farming folk. Here is his telephone number. I asked Steve to see about Campbell and Dawson."

Steve said "Dawson is now the assistant stationmaster at Middlesborough. He is coming to Doncaster this Sunday for a three day conference about the Beeching cuts. He will come to the police station at 4pm after he has settled into his hotel room. Still having problems trying to find Campbell but he didn't continue with the army after his National Service."

"Jack anything from the wood?"

No, Reg gave us a mug shot of Stewart and we asked a few people if they had seen this man in the wood nothing. Dad rang Frank Edwards and he said that he and George would like to pay for Stewart's funeral they know Elsie is brassic and they are willing to give her a job as a cleaner at the bookies, Tina is at the Chapel of Rest with Elsie and will tell her."

"Righto. I would like you to continue with the wood and ask about vehicles being driven through the there perhaps a change of shift tomorrow night sit up in the plain car where you can see the shack then a late shift on Sunday same thing. I am off tomorrow but Frank I believe is around."

17
The Stationmaster

Sunday,
24th April 1966

Renton arrived at the station at 10am and in his in tray found 6 large files with a note from Chief Inspector Fox "Ralph, sorry to give you these files but I am now on my hols and will be until 17th May, so over to you." Frank had warned him when he first arrived in Doncaster to watch out for Fox who was known as a duck shoveller meaning he would try to pass on work. Renton looked at the file headings and saw that the last date for them to be submitted to the court prosecutor was 27th April. By 11am he had sorted out two of them and decided he needed a strong mug of coffee.

He went down to the collators, found Frank there. He made himself a coffee and told Frank about the files.

"I bet they are bulky. But no worries I have booked us two slots at the Red Lion for 12.15. Roast Lamb for you and pork for me."

"Aha forward planning you will go far young man."

Frank said "Yesterday I had a walk through Sandall Beat Wood from the old gate to the hut, it is a dark place and perfect for what the killer wanted. Oh here is Doc Wells report for Stewart. Looking at the professional way they were killed I presume the torture was to find out something as opposed for pleasure."

"I rang Mr. Duggan apparently he is a pig breeder not a pig farmer, apparently there is a difference. He got quite shirty when I told him I was a copper, he assumed I was investigating his son's death."

"What eleven years later. When are you seeing him?"

"Monday 12 midday with Steve."

"What time is the stationmaster getting here?"

"3pm."

Later they went to the Red Lion and enjoyed their meals and a pint.

Back in the collators the Front Office rang at ten to three to say Mr. Dawson had arrived. Frank went down and introduced himself, took him to the new interview room and introduced him to Renton.

Renton said "Do you mind if my colleague makes a few notes?"

"No please do."

"I see after your training at Catterick you were posted to Suez?"

"No, I did the training. But because I was an almost trained accountant they posted me to Berlin and put me in the orderly office with a creature called Cooper. Typical army when I was demobbed my papers said thank you for your service in Egypt."

"So did you go out and do the perimeter duties?"

"No purely admin, which suited me. Have you ever been to Germany in the winter it is very cold."

"So what can you tell us about Carlyle and his cronies?"

"Bully boys and Carlyle was the worst and he had brains unlike the others. Cooper was put in the orderly office as my "assistant" he was a snidey creature.I caught him going through some of the military despatches, God knows what he got up to when I wasn't there."

"Were the dispatches solely military?"

"Mostly, they were colour coded and we had other than British stuff American and French. Some of the dispatches were very sensitive especially the stuff about the Russians. My job was simply to send them on to whoever they were addressed to. We used army despatch riders. Once I had seen inside the cover I would seal them and then give them to the despatch chaps."

"Did you see much of Alistair Duggan in Berlin?"

"Yes nice lad, clever."

"Do you think there was anything untoward about his death?"

"Well there were rumours. He confided in me that he thought Carlyle was passing information to someone on the other side. You know the East Germans. I warned him about Carlyle being a snake."

"Do you mean spying?"

"Well passing on stuff he may have got from Cooper or another source maybe."

"Did you tell anyone up the chain about this?"

"I had no real proof apart from Cooper and the dispatches. We are talking about the army here it could be very unwise to start throwing any accusations about others. I warned Alistair to be careful who he talked to. After he lost his stripe he changed a fair bit. More guarded in barracks where he went in his spare time I have no idea."

"Why did he confide in you?"

"My dad and his had been in the paras."

"Did he confide in anyone else?"

"He said that he had confided in some chap in the RMP who was working undercover. I told him to keep that to himself. After he lost his stripe he started following Carlyle when he went into Berlin. Al had met a woman from England who worked in a club and she gave him some information about what was going on in there. The club was owned by a German with a partner who was apparently in the military at the same barracks as Carlyle."

"Do you know who that was?"

"Al said it was a cook."

"Did he say who?"

"No he died before he could tell me."

"Thank you for that, here is my card, if you think of anything else relevant please call me. Is your father and Alistair's still in touch.?"

"No my father was killed in Korea. When Alistair died I heard the gun explode and went into the barrack room to find Horton holding him and screaming for a medic. I tried to stop the bleeding but it was useless most of his face had gone. The medics arrived and took over Horton was a gibbering idiot at the best of times but he was useless. Afterwards I spoke to Jim and Fred and Fred was of the opinion it was a set up. Cooper didn't show, Stewart was nowhere to be seen and Carlyle was out doing the perimeter guard. Apart from Horton all the people who had caused Ali grief in training and in Germany were absent."

Renton said "Could Steve just take a statement about that last bit. Can I get you a cup of tea perhaps?"

"No that's fine."

After the statement Frank showed him out.

In the collators Frank said "Sounds so like a set up and the main contenders apart from Horton were nowhere to be seen,"

18
The Pig Breeder

Reg and Frank were in the collators.
Frank said "It is 8.30am and I reckon he will smell that kettle on and be here now."

Reg was about to reply when Renton walked in. Reg produced a coffee.

"Excellent timing" said Renton

Reg said "So what is the plan today?"

Renton said "Brampton for Steve and I, Frank to morning prayers, Jack and Tina Sandall Wood see if there are any walkers who might have seen a vehicle and you Reg anything on Carlyle and Campbell try Scotland Yard see if they have a criminal record also the others on that list that we haven't already found or interviewed. Also can you contact Smudge we need to find where Horton is living and have a word."

Reg produced a map of Lincolnshire and pointed out where Brampton was. Steve arrived Reg beckoned him over and pointed out Brampton "I take it you are the navigator Steve?"

Steve said "We have the Inspector's very comfortable plain car, I have fuelled it up and ready when you are sir." He handed the keys to Renton. He looked at the map "Bartholomew's map of Licolnshire which looks as if it has seen better days."

Reg said "That's what happens on a cycling holiday when you suddenly get caught out in a thunderstorm, young man. How many maps do you know have a netting on the back to keep them intact."

"You are a cyclist?" Steve said in an amazed voice.

"Once upon a time when I was a carefree young and chasing girls."

"You had to use a bike to catch them as they ran away."

"Take him away before I physically explain the Marquess of Queensbury's Rules."

As they drove out of the police yard Steve said "I cannot image Mrs Prestleigh on a bicycle she is a bit on the large side."

Renton said "I think the cycling was pre-Mrs Prestleigh. Open that map, find the A638 and us heading for Austerfield."

"Ah yes Austerfield the home of William Bradford."

"Yes so I am told was he a villain or fleeing justice."

"Neither, William Bradford was the leader of the Pilgrim Fathers and founded Plymouth in America he was the Governor for nearly 30 years."

"I am surrounded by such knowledgeable people." Said Renton.

"My dad, history teacher and a collector of anything to do with Yorkshire, if you ever meet him do not ask him about the Yorkshire cricket team he will bore you rigid."

"His son's not doing a bad job map please."

"A631 to Gainsborough then a right onto the A156 to Torksey famous for the Vikings but before that we will get to Brampton."

"Righto if we make good time we could go into Lincoln and sniff out a bacon sandwich."

Sure enough two bacon sandwiches and two coffees later they were driving through the flatlands of Lincolnshire they could smell the pigs before they got to the farm. Renton slammed the brakes on as a tractor pulled out of field in front of them. Renton got out of the car.

"Can you tell us where Duggan's Farm is?" he said to the tractor driver.

He said "Yes down the road, follow me I'm Alexander Duggan."

They followed, he turned into a gate then into a large courtyard, they followed and parked.

"You're the coppers are you dad's a bit narky today."

They followed him between a couple of barn's he turned off pointing to a parking space next to a patio next to th farmhouse. They found an older man sitting in a wheelchair and a young woman sitting next to him.

"Dad a couple of coppers for you?"

"Yes you have come to tell me who killed my son, I hope."

Renton introduced Steve and himself and they showed their ID cards.

"Mr Duggan tell me about your son's death."

He motioned them to sit down.

"You mean what I know about the shambles of a cock-up by the army not properly investigating his murder did I say properly."

Can you tell us what you know I understand your son knew his way around weapons?"

"Yes that's true, he was set up you know?"

"By whom?"

"Carlyle, Stewart, Cooper and Horton and don't forget that bloody cook Kowalski, the biggest crook of them all."

"So why murder him."

"Because of what he knew, what he had found out about them, he wrote me every week, he said they were giving information to the Russians."

"Why didn't he pass that information on to his superiors."

"My son was very methodical, he was looking at the bigger picture and when he was ready he would have done, but they finished him off before he could do that."

"He was cleaning a weapon when it blew up in his face."

"I cannot believe that his weapon would have been in disrepair."

"It wasn't his weapon, it apparently jammed and he was trying to clear it for someone else."

"Bloody hell they gave him someone else's weapon, bloody Carlyle I have no doubt, sneaky bastard."

It was a cleaning parade before they went out on guard duty they worked in pairs checking each other's weapon."

"Set up." said Alexander Duggan.

"Yes, did you contact the army after he had died."

"Yes for all the good it did, just a letter nothing else."

"Renton said "Although I am very interested in finding your son's killer we think that it could be the same man who has murdered two people in Doncaster. Both men were in the same intake as your son an Eric Cooper and a Terence Stewart."

"Well bloody good riddance, bastards, no loss to society either of them. You should be looking for Carlyle or the bloody cook."

"What makes you say that?"

"Listen mainly Cooper but no doubt Horton and Stewart were selling information to the bloody commies. They passed it onto that creep Carlyle who passed it to his commie mates."

"Can you tell me where you and your son were on 13th April and the 21st April?"

"Haha that's a good one Inspector you think we would waste our time bumping off your two commies. We were sorting nearly 300 pigs. I don't know if you have noticed I am not the most mobile of people and Alex works from 6 in the morning until midnight. So I think it is time you left."

Renton gave his card to Duggan "If you want to talk to me at anytime about anything in relation to your son's death and it brings you and me closer to catching this killer then call me."

"Aye."

Driving back, once away from the farmhouse Renton said "So Steve what do you think about that conversation?"

Steve said "A bitter man understandably, the son is a big sod he looks capable of murder. But didn't someone say that Ali regularly wrote to his dad so any information he had he passed to dad. I bet he still has all those letters. We need to see them."

"Yes I think the old man knows more than he is letting on and it would be good to find out what the son's letters were on about. But we cannot force him, we need him to come to us which I think he will eventually. I think the son Alex might persuade him. I need a sandwich, let's go into Gainsborough I know a bakery there."

"How do you know all these places?"

"When I joined up in 1939 I was posted to the Intelligence Corps and there was a panic in 1940 that Hitler was planning to invade us.

After Dunkirk the panic increased. Initially I was going to be posted abroad but I had an injury. So I was in a team that looked at the defences on the east coast. Although everyone thought that Jerry would come across the Channel, the brains thought he might come across from Holland. So we looked at the coast from Tyneside to the Humber Estuary and 20 miles inland. Once my wrist was healed I was posted abroad.

19
The Letter

They went to Gainsborough enjoyed a couple of sandwiches and a drink. Renton pointed out a telephone box to Steve "Give Reg a ring, see if anything is happening over there?"

Steve went to the box and then came back." You must have a sixth sense. After we left Helen Duggan convinced the old man that his only way of finding out what happened to the son was to cosy up to us. I asked Reg to ring them back and said we would return."

"Excellent, go back in the bakers and buy that small Victoria Sponge as a peace offering."

Back at the farm they presented the cake to Helen.

Duggan said "Helen love put the kettle on and let's have a drink and a slice of cake."

They sat down and Duggan said "You are my only hope of finding out what happened to Alistair. I'm sorry I was a bit shirty earlier apart from my injuries, I now have arthritis. As I said before Alistair wrote to us regularly. He didn't trust the mail in the barracks so he would post the letters from a post office in Berlin. However he posted this one in the married quarters and I wonder if someone intercepted it."He produced a letter and said "This is the last letter we received the X stands for Kowalski and the P is for Oskar Peplinski who was a sergeant in the RMP and working undercover."

The letter said "Dear Dad, hope all is well on the farm. I now know that X and his boys are passing information to a person in the den." (The den was the Blue Iguana Club) "I think the other owner was or is a Stasi officer. X is in charge of organising the banquets for the top brass both military and civilian in and outside the barracks I think he has set some of them up to blackmail for info or perhaps money. I intend to blow them wide open when I am demobbed with the help of P. Love to Helen and Alex.

Alex said "Helen's best friend is the librarian in Lincoln and I asked her if she could trace the name Kowalski. There is only one he is or was a Professor at Cambridge University, Henryk Kowalski."

"So how old do you think this cook is?"

Duggan said "40 to 50."

"Righto Mr Duggan, thank you for the tea and I will be in touch. I will contact the Military Police if necessary through the Attorney General and do some digging."

They all shook hands.

On the way back Renton said "We need to find this Kowlski and the Prof, we will get the bloodhound called Reg on it. If someone intercepted the letter and told Kowalski then I should think he is long gone."

20
Harold Crowley

Renton arrived at his usual time looked at his desk calendar Tuesday 26th April 1966, he got stuck into the files on his desk, one for GBH and one for criminal damage. He did a quick read through them but knew that they would be all in order because they had been signed up by Frank. He looked at his watch, nearly 10 am so Frank would be almost finished at morning prayers so it was time for a strong coffee in the collators. In the collators he found Steve telling Frank and Reg about their trip to Brampton. He made himself a mug of coffee.

Reg said "I might be able to track Kowalski through the Army Catering Corps, but Peplinski is a different kettle of fish the RMP are notoriously reticent about giving up details about their own."

"What about the two lads who helped us with Bond Neil and Alex wasn't it." said Frank.

"Yes good one can you do that Reg Sheffield City Police." said Renton.

Just then Dennis Parkin came in "Body found in a house in Bentley. Local bobby forced the front door. Apparently the owner hasn't been seen for a while body on the bed upstairs lot of blood. I have the car ready boss."

Renton said "Reg ring Doc Wells and Peter Johns, where in Bentley then Dennis?"

"Broughton Avenue."

"Righto let's go and you Steve. Reg get hold of Jack and Tina. I will see them there."

At the house the local constable introduced himself and saluted.

"Morning sir I am PC Barlow."

"Good morning I am told you had to force the door to get in?"

"Postman normally hands the post to the owner, but there hasn't been some post for him for a while today he had a letter for him and knocked but no answer. Postie looked through the letter box and saw a newspaper lying on the floor and an awful smell. He got someone at the Post Office to ring me."

"What time was that?"

"Five past nine, sir."

"And then?"

"I came here had a look through the letterbox smelt like raw meat in a butchers, the neighbour Winnie Armitage said she hasn't seen him for a while so I put the door in had a look in each room, called out usual thing then found him in the bedroom, dead."

"Do you know his name?"

"Yes sir Harold Crowley.

"Very good, I am going in for a look, no one to enter except Doctor Wells and DO Peters our fingerprint officer."

"Very good sir."

Renton went in everything was very neat and quite spartan as he went upstairs he encountered the flies. He had a quick look at the body and noticed that his throat looked like the other victims. He opened the window to get the bluebottles out. He went back downstairs and found the back door unlocked and found Jack standing there.

"Steve and Tina have started house to house. Thought I would have a look round the back. No lock on the back gate."

Leaving the back door open Renton went back upstairs into the bathroom saw blood in the sink also a bloody footprint on the floor. He opened the window. He went back in the bedroom the victim was lying on the bed with his ankles tied together with rope and were at the head end of the bed. His hands were tied with rope and his head was hanging over the bed. He walked back to the door just as Doc Wells appeared.

Doctor Wells went in had a look at the body. "Well and truly dead."

"Garrotted do you think?"

"That is possible but the post mortem will determine that, my chaps are on their way. Peter is downstairs I will tell him to come up."I will take a swab of that and compare it with the body. Will let you know time of death after the pm rough guess within the last couple of days I will write the death certificate now."

Peter arrived

Renton said "There is a bloody footprint in the bathroom so if you can photograph that for us."

Peter went in the bathroom and said "I reckon that is a size 11 or maybe 12."He took some photographs then said "There is blood on the towel hanging on the door I will bag that up and take a sample for Doctor Wells."

Renton watched Peter put what looked like a sheet of paper over the footprint and then using a small roller pressed the paper onto the footprint he then put the paper in a cellophane envelope.

"Righto Peter I will leave it to you and when you have finished send up the Doc's merry men to get the body."

Renton went down to the back door and said to Jack "I am going to lock this door anything untoward in the garden. Do you know PC Barlow?

"Nothing here, Nobby Barlow solid good local bobby well liked. Dad rated him but he is ex Marines."

Renton went to the front door and said "PC Barlow did you know the victim well?"

"Well enough, he was a cook, breakfast chef part-time in Doncaster at the Danum a sort of relief cook. From the way he dressed I would say he had a few bob. He did some cooking at the Miners Institute for the down and outs and poorer sorts also the WW Club?"

"The WW Club?"

"Yes it's the Widows and Widowers club, it's for retired folk mainly miners and suchlike giving them a meal at Christmas and Easter a roast and a raffle."

"Was he a local man?"

"No a southerner, once told me he was from Cambridge."

"Single or married?"

"Single, had a cleaner come in every couple of weeks, relative of Mrs Armitage next door. She is a curtain twitcher knows everyone's business. Your WPC should have a chat with her."

"Thanks for that."As he turned Peter came to the door."

"Any fingerprints?"

"Yes sir 3 separate sets."

"He had a cleaner."

"Right, we need to see her. There are no prints on the taps where he washed himself, probably cleaned them off with the towel."

Just then the mortuary team arrived.

"Upstairs" said Peter "I will continue here sir see what I can find cannot find a murder weapon neither blade or wire."

The mortuary team came down with the familiar box. One of them Jake said to Renton."We have left him tied up I'm sure the Doc will let you know if the rope is the same as the last one."

"Thank you Jake." Renton said to Jack "When Peter had finished we will go in and give the house a search. Anywhere for a cuppa round here Pc Barlow?"

"Yes sir just up the road near the post office is the police box, I have the makings in there."

"Guard the door, when Peter has finished we will come back and search the house."

He said "How long Peter?

"Maybe 45 minutes sir."

Renton and Jack went to the Police Box and had a coffee. Later they were back at the house just as Peter was leaving, they went inside and closed the door.

Jack said "What are we looking for?"

"Anything with his name on it bills driving documents birth certificate passport.?"

They looked around the living room no pictures no ornaments but quite a few books. Two armchairs a coffee table a sideboard with a wireless on but no television. The kitchen was spotlessly clean and had 2 of everything plates, cups, saucers and cutlery. A couple of pans, Jack picked up the mail and opened it all on the work surface. Mainly bills and a letter from the Miners institute.

Jack said "It is very clean in here and all the utensils are spotless."

Renton said "He was a cook and worked at the Danum."

Upstairs in the small bedroom it had a desk, a chair and a small fold-up bed. On the desk was a bottle of vodka half full and 2 glasses that had been used all covered in Peter's dusting powder. Jack opened the vodka and sniffed it.

"Bloody hell that is strong, I reckon that is moonshine especially as there is no label on the bottle."

"Where would you get moonshine in Yorkshire it's not exactly Kentucky.?"

"There is a rumour that a farmer near Brierley brews his own out of potatoes."

"Bring that chair let's have a look in the attic."Renton gave him a torch.

Jack stood on the chair and moved the attic door out of the way."Aha what have we hear."
He passed down a suitcase and then another.

Renton took them into the small bedroom and onto the desk moving the bottle and glasses. He opened the first case and pulled something out and gave it to Jack "Do you recognise this?"

"Well well our old friend the officers despatch bag."He opened it and pulled out a wad of English money in a roll with an elastic band around it. Also inside was a passport in the name of Harold Crowley. Renton pulled out another despatch bag and opened it and pulled out a wad of American dollars and another passport with Crowley's photograph in but no details in it.

Renton said "Let's take these suitcases to the station and look into the other one and get Peter to photograph the contents." They went downstairs to find a carpenter repairing the door.

PC Barlow said "My cousin sir."

"Very good PC Barlow when he has finished I want you to lock the door. The back door is locked here is the key. There are 2 sets of keys for this door. You keep one and we will keep one because we may be coming back ok. Do you live in Bentley?"

"Yes I do sir."

"Write your statement about what has happened here today and can you pay a passing attention to the house."

Jack took the cases to the car and Renton found Steve, "Anything?"

"Not a lot apart from cooking in the Miners Institute he was a very private person."

"Righto, he apparently worked as a relief at the Danum so go there now and ask about him and also see Dick in the Diner see if he knew him. We will see you back at the station.

21
Leslie is a man

Renton and Jack went back to the station and went into the collators and found Frank making a cuppa. Jack put the suitcases in the exhibits locker.

"Ralph can you go and see the Chief he just wants the bare bones of the murder but wait a while Benson is in there."

"Does Benson know he is retired, as soon as Peter has taken Crowley's prints I want Ted Ramsden to run them to Scotland Yard and find out who he really is. He has a passport with his photograph in it but no name. Also we need to get house to house going I will have a word with the Chief and get some of our local lads out there."

"I will see Inspector Walker and get some constables out on the ground maybe David and Tina can go with them and take any statements." said Frank.

Renton then told him and Reg about the suitcases and their contents."Once the council have cleaned up the house we will go back and take the house apart. I looked through what paperwork he had and there was no evidence of a bank or any savings accounts."

Reg said "Steve just rang with the telephone number for Leslie Reid."

"Excellent" said Renton, he continued "Dennis can you ring the cleaner then see her and have a chat and get a statement, the last time she saw Crowley. Did you get a statement from the postman?"

"Of course and I picked one up from PC Barlow."

Reg said "I have tracked down a Kowalski but he was a Professor at Cambridge University. So I had a chat with their librarian. Henryk Kowalski escaped from Warsaw ahead of the Nazis came to England with a letter of introduction to teach at the university. Once war broke out he was channelled into a government unit something to do with disinformation and certain secret units authorised by Churchill. The Professor died in 1960 aged 81. Not sure about a wife or children."

"That's a start what about Peplinski any luck there?"

"Not a lot so far."

"Righto I will see if the coast is clear and see the Chief."

30 minutes later he returned followed by Peter and Ted Ramsden. Renton gave Howell's prints to Ted "Straight away to Scotland Yard Reg has contacted their fingerprint bureau and emphasized the importance of checking them soon as. For the rest of us debrief at 4pm."

4pm arrived Renton briefly explained about PC Barlow forcing the door and then said "I have had a telephone conversation with Doctor Wells in his inimitable fashion what." Everyone laughed. He continued "Crowley was tied up with rope but not the same as that used on Stewart but can be bought from any hardware shop. His throat was slit with a heavy blade thicker than a carving knife. Also he died within four days of him being found. He had damage to the back of his head and looks like a downward blow to stun him so he could then be tied up. Peter found two clear sets of fingerprints and a third but were very slightly smeared possibly by the vodka but Peter thinks he might be able to get a clear print. Two are everywhere so Crowley and possibly the cleaner. The third smeared set are only on one glass of two. So presumably Crowley may have known his killer, they shared a glass of vodka and then the killer struck him. It' possible he may have tortured him. Steve what have you got?"

Steve said "Not a lot, he was the relief chef at the Danum Hotel. He told the other chef he didn't need the money but he liked to keep his hand in. He said he had a pension and was always very smart when he turned up to do the cooking."

"He had met Dick in the Diner but he was too expensive for Dick. The staff at the Miners Institute thought the sun shone out of his lunchbox. Apparently all the food he purchased and would pay half the cost himself saying he would be old one day."

"Dennis what have you got?"

"Lesley Reid is spelt Leslie because he is a man. I think there was much more going on with them other than just cleaning. When I told him Crowley was dead he burst into tears and said "My poor Harold." Let him get over the shock and let Tina have a sisterly type chat with him. I think he would open up to a woman. He did say that he and Harold had been a couple for a while, but Crowley had called time on it but they were still friends. Last time he saw him was about 3 weeks ago early April."

He turned to David and Tina "anything from house to house?"

"No but a lot of people were at work when we were there I suggest we try again maybe tomorrow from 4pm to 10pm." said Tina

"Excellent good idea if you can pass that on to Inspector Walker and his lads. Jack can you get the cases out of the locker and lets all have a look at the contents."

Jack put the suitcases on the table and emptied the contents on the table when they had all had a look Renton said "Any thoughts anyone."

Frank said "Ready to run to a new life."

"Exactly. Mr Crowley is not the person his neighbours think he is. We shall continue this tomorrow but 6pm in the Red Lion usual rules. Don't forget pocket book entries at all times."

22
Nobby

Renton arrived at the station and went to his office, only one more file and then Fox can do anymore that come in. Frank came and said "Can you go and see the Chief before prayers, he just buttonholed me outside his office. Apparently Benson has been bending his ear about a serial killer. The Chief thinks perhaps the press have been getting at Benson."

"Righto see you in later the collators."

20 minutes later Renton arrived in the collators. Reg made him a mug of strong coffee.

"Thanks Reg I need this."

All the team were there. Renton said "Benson said to the Chief that he may have let slip that he thought the murders were the work of a serial killer. So the Chief made Benson ring the editor of the post there and then and say he had made a mistake and say that it is not a serial killer and the public are not in any danger because the killer used an unusual technique not seen before."

Reg said "I bet that made Benson sweat, I am liking our Chief more and more I thought Benson was now retired."

"The Chief has said to the Editor that when the killer is arrested and remember it is only 2 weeks since the first murder they will get the first bite of the cherry and he said if the Post deviate from that line they will be in the kak. I did ask Benson why he is the only person in the West Riding who doesn't know he is retired. He said he was there on a consultancy basis."

Ted Ramsden walked in and said "Reg is that kettle working."This was Ted's way of asking for a mug of tea.

Renton said to Ted "How did you get on at the Yard."

"Usual arrogance me being a hick copper, but I went straight to their fingerprint chap. Ex marine so no problem there. He is going to check Crowley's prints and the print on the padlock. I have given him your number and yours Reg."

"You had better get off home and get some shuteye."

"Not a problem got back last night, gave the Inspector's car a bit of a workout."

"Excellent. PC Barlow rang last night to say that the council cleaners will be finished by 11 today so once Frank is back from prayers we and Peter will go to the house and see if we can find anything relevant. Jack and Tina go and have a chat to the cleaner, ask him if there is anything of Howell's that he would like to remember him by. Bring Reid to the house for 12.30, Ted I understand you know PC Barlow, he has quite a posh accent for a Tyke."

"Nobby Barlow of Bentley"

"Nobby?"

"His dad was Lieutenant Colonel St John Barlow, Coldstream Guards, circa the trenches of the Western Front a genuine blue blood."

"Really and he is only a constable."

"Had the posh education, went a bit to the left and turned his back on all that stuff. Daddy expected him to join the Guards in the Second War, he enlisted in the Royal Engineers refused a commission got to sergeant and became a committed socialist. His older brother Montague became a Guards officer died at Monte Cassino. The father was a firebrand and was badly wounded at the Somme and berated the medical staff for not getting him back on his feet he apparently said he had to get back and start biffing the Boche."

"So daddy wasn't happy with son number 2."

"No but when he died he left a considerable sum to Nobby who along with his socialist ideals gave most it to the British Legion and other charities such as the Widows and Orphans."

Renton said "Steve can you go to the mortuary get Howell's clothes and the ropes and exhibit them. I have not seen Austin is he okay."

"He has gone to Portsmouth RMLI reunion a three day event so it will take him another three days to recover."

Frank came back from prayers and then with Peter they went to Bentley.

In the house they went upstairs and Frank had a look in the loft but apart from some paint tins it was empty. While Renton looked through the wardrobe, Frank went to the fireplace, he pulled the wooden cover off and in the place where the grate should be was a small wooden box. He called Peter who took it out and checked for fingerprints. Frank then opened it and pulled out a small leather bag, he opened it and gently poured out the contents a very expensive looking pocket watch and 3 diamonds about the size of an acorn each.

Renton said to Peter "can you take a photograph of the diamonds and the watch?"

Renton said "My dad had a watch like that if it is German it is worth a mint."He opened the back "Yep it's German alright." He put the watch and the diamonds back in the bag. Frank took out a couple of black and white photographs. One showed 5 men in a line, the middle one was a younger version of Crowley's passport photograph.

Renton said "I wonder if this is the gang."He looked on the back it said "Me and the boys with Vlad."

Renton said "Vlad is Russian and short for Vladimir."

The other photograph showed an elderly man in a suit and an elderly woman and on the back was the word "Rodzic."

Frank looked at the photo "London you can see Big Ben in the distance, this must be mum and dad."

Peter came in and said "I cannot find anything extra from my last visit. There is a small shed in the back garden but just tools."

"Ok Peter." said Renton " Can you wait until the cleaner turns up then you can take his prints for elimination then go back to the station and we will see you later."

Renton and Frank went into the kitchen just as Jack and Tina brought in Leslie Reid, Frank gave the nod to Jack and he and Tina withdrew into the lounge.

Renton introduced himself and Frank."Leslie is there anything of Harold's that you would like as a memento?"

He looked very near to tears "Harold had a small leather bag with a pocket watch that belonged to his father he said I could have it, if anything happened to him."

"Yes of course." he motioned to Frank who pulled the watch out of the bag with the fob and gave it to Reid.

"Could I have the bag?"

"I am afraid not Leslie we need to keep that for evidential purposes. However I need you to sign my pocketbook to show that we have given you the watch" said Frank.

They could see the disappointment on his face. Frank then made an entry in his book and Reid signed it. Reid then produced a document and gave it to Renton saying "This is Harold's will, there is a solicitor in Doncaster who has the original could you give this one to him. Harold said that he wanted the house to be sold and the money halved and half to Mrs Armitage and the other half to me."

Renton said "Yes of course we will deliver it to the solicitor" He then said "This is Peter our fingerprint chap he would like to take your fingerprints just for elimination purposes is that alright with you."

Reid said "Yes of course."

Peter took him into the kitchen and explained the procedure.

15 minutes later Renton said to him "Are you okay would you like a lift home?"

"Er is that possible."

"Yes of course." he turned to Jack and Tina "Could you take Mister Reid home please." He winked at Tina.

When he had gone Frank said "Greedy little sod he knew those diamonds were in with the watch and he and auntie are cleaning up on the money from the house."

"What say we get the bus back via the Diner what do you think is on the menu today."

"Toad in the hole, mash peas and that lovely gravy followed by bananas and custard."

23
Debrief

After the culinary delights of the Diner, Renton and Frank were in the collators showing Reg the diamonds and said about Reid's disappointed face.

Reg said "He owns a bungalow and gets half the house what a crying shame."

Renton was looking at the 2 photographs and said "The word Rodzic what language do you reckon that is?"

Frank said "Maybe Russian, Polish maybe Czech."

Reg said "Wait a mo." he picked up the telephone and rang someone."Polish for father or sire."

Frank said "I know this sounds daft but I reckon Crowley was Polish, bloody hell I bet he is Kowalski. No but hang on a minute Crowley is in the middle of those 5 blokes and it mentions Vlad which is not exactly an English name."

Just then Reg's phone rang he picked it up "Yes yes sir but he is dead and in Doncaster mortuary. Yes I understand I think you need to talk to our SIO he is here."He passed the receiver to Renton.

Renton said "Yes, yes I am Detective Superintendent Renton the SIO, yes the very same. Tomorrow eleven very good, in the collators I will be here." He put the receiver down. That was Detective Chief Superintendent William S Bullstone of the Metropolitan Police Special Branch stroke Foreign Affairs. The last time I met him he was Major WS Bullstone Intel Corps several weeks after D-Day."

"Big cheese, I know that name." said Reg.

"He is coming here tomorrow, he was under the impression Crowley was in the cells and wanted to interrogate him. The fingerprints Ted took to his chum in the Yard show that Crowley is actually Henryk

Kowalski the son of Professor Kowalski. Kowalski alias Crowley is wanted on espionage charges including treason blackmail and theft."

"Well they won't be locking him up in Wormwood Scrubs." said Frank.

30 minutes later and everyone was present so Renton told them about Reid and the news about Crowley being Kowalski. He then said "Ted anything from Nobby?"

"Yes he had a regular cup of tea and biscuits with Mrs Armitage. Crowley was seen as a good egg. As we know he did his bit at the Miners Institute for the WW Club and at Christmas and Easter. Also he helped out at the Polish Servicemen's club in Hull. About 3 months ago he had a visit from 2 men, all seemed very jolly, Crowley would leave the back door open and she could hear the clinking of glasses and singing and toasting each other. But 2 weeks before he disappeared she heard him speaking loudly saying "No more you bastards, no more." She wasn't sure whether he was actually talking to someone or if he was on the telephone. She said that she knew that Crowley and her nephew had been quite close for quite a while."

"Righto Tina Jack did you get a chance to talk to dear Leslie?"

Tina said "He met Crowley in Cambridge after the war Crowley was on leave, they had a brief affair and then Crowley went back to Germany. They stayed in touch and then about 5 years ago they met and continued their relationship. They would occasionally go to Cambridge for a weekend, Crowley always paid for everything. Apparently Crowley didn't like banks. Even the Danum paid him in cash."

"Yes of course you have to give the bank your life story to get an account. Now I have the report from the Doc and he is now of the mind that Crowley was killed with either the double wire in a messy fashion or it could have been a heavy blade. Time of death is somewhere between the 14th to the 19th April somewhere in that 5 day gap."

Frank said "So he was killed in between Cooper and Stewart, all within two weeks he certainly wasn't hanging around although I think we have two killers here. Crowleys wasn't as neat as the other two."

Renton said "Yes my thoughts as well let's leave it at that and prepare for the typhoon that is William S Bullstone."

24
Special Branch

Renton arrived at his desk at 9am to find a postcard on his desk from Robert Bond. He looked on the back it said "Lovely weather here could be worse you could be living in China." This was a reference to the cultural revolution that had taken place 10 days before. Renton normally tore them up but decided as this was handwritten to keep it. He then went to see the Chief about the visit of Bullstone. 30 minutes later he was in the collators waiting for the others to arrive. Within five minutes everyone was there and made themselves a drink.

Reg said "Is this going to be a private meeting or are we all invited?"

"If I have my way it will be here for us all to hear."

At 11am Frank brought him in. DCS Bullstone was an imposing 6'4" 50 years of age with a large Roman nose and a trim sergeant majors moustache. The parting in his hair looked liked it had been done with a razorblade and he had piercing steely blue eyes. Steve thought he looked like an eagle looking for its next meal.

Bullstone waved them all to sit down and walked up to Reg and said "Long time Reginald good to see you." They shook hands, he then turned to Renton and said "And you Lieutenant Renton." They shook hands. He then pulled out a sheet of paper from his briefcase and said "I am sure you have all signed the Official Secrets Act but what I am about to tell you needs you all to put down your name rank and number with your date of birth and where born, then sign it."

"That won't be necessary." said Renton "I can vouch for everyone in this room and only I need to sign." He then filled in the form, signed it and passed it back to Bullstone who put it back in his briefcase.

"When I saw the fingerprint form and was informed it was actually Henryk Kowalski I was over the moon. I have been after this bastard for 8 years. His actual surname is Bialek the son of Professor Bialek.

But they took the name Kowalski when they arrived in England to protect his father. He is wanted for treason, spying also blackmail and theft by the Americans and French authorities. When I saw the fingerprints for Cooper and Stewart I was hoping they would lead me to Kowalski but blow me down they are dead as well."

Renton showed him the photograph of the five and the name Vlad.

"Yes Vladimir Sokolov his contact. Sokol is Russian for falcon and that was his contact name."

Frank said "So Kowalski is wanted by the French and Americans?"

"Oh my goodness yes, the secrets he has passed onto his contact were all about what they intended to happen along with the British Government in the future and of course we now have the Berlin Wall."

Jack said "How did you find out about all this?"

"In 1958 Kowalski and Sokolov vanished from Germany. The club they jointly owned the Blue Iguana was burnt to the ground. The powers that be were on the verge of arresting them both. They had been setting up the top brass from the French and American Military using attractive women as a lure then giving them drinks with a little something in and then photographing them in compromising situations with the women and men. The payoff was information and money. In 1960 Vladimir came to England and gave himself up because the Russians were eliminating some of there agents in a clear-up. He told us everything implicating Kowalski and to a certain extent a Derek Carlyle."

Renton said "We would like to get a hold of Carlyle."

"Yes so would I, he may have killed your victims. We have had information from an undercover sergeant in the RMP Oskar Peplinski who in turn had received info from a young soldier in 1955 Private Alistair Duggan, who died in Germany."

"Duggan was set up by Carlyle."

"Yes indirectly with the help of Stewart and possibly a Gerald Horton. The army at the time closed ranks and covered it up. We had had a whisper about Carlyle and the link to Kowalski so the Attorney general and the Home Office shall we say discussed what had happened to young Duggan and we got the truth about the rifle being rigged to back fire on Duggan. They had kept the rifle and we had an expert look it over."

"I promised Mr Duggan I would help him find the truth out about his son's death."

"Yes and you can by getting that degenerate Carlyle to spill the beans when you get him. However I am meeting Mr Duggan at 3pm today and will tell him everything about his son's death and why it was hushed up."

So what is Kowalski's background?"

"Professor Bialek held the chair for sciences at Warsaw University but he and several other boffins could see the way the wind was blowing with the Nazi's so they skipped. The others went to America but Bialek came to England with his wife Elena who was Jewish and his son also called Henryk. They were lodged in Cambridge University. They changed their name to Kowalski to stop any action against them by Nazi sympathisers. MI6 had acquired a document well before 1939 which was a list of people who could be of a use to the Nazis it also said that those who did not conform would be shot. In 1940 Professor Bialek was seconded to an organisation within the War Chamber to outfox the Nazi's. Around this time the son enlisted in the army and was drafted into the Army Catering Corps. After the war he stayed in the army in Berlin and somewhere along the way he became pro Russian. Dad was a very upright solid patriotic man who hated the Nazi's. His son however was a venal and corrupt degenerate. By the by Ralph your father was involved in an investigation that involved pro Nazis in London."

"Yes dad did say he had a bellyful of them and it was so pleasant to get on with detecting real criminals after the war."

"There is one thing you can do for me and it might help your situation. Peplinski is now a DS in Hull where he is wasting away. I have had a word with your Chief and he has said you could do with another DS. He will be arriving on Monday 2nd May, next week. Here is my direct line."

He handed Renton his card and then turned to Reg "Cheerio Reginald keep propping this lot up."

With a wave of his hand he was gone.

Reg said to Renton "Why did you put that number 31 after your signature?"

"He will give that to his secretary and she will wonder what the 31 is. She will point it out to him but his arrogance won't allow him to ask me. He will give her some bogus reply and then it will nag at him."

They all laughed and then Renton said to Reg "What was that all about Reginald?"

"I joined Doncaster Constabulary but the Mets wanted a fresh face looking chap to go undercover, someone from the sticks and unknown in London. I met Inspector Bullstone who was the officer in charge of all that stuff. They were trying to root out pro German and Russian sympathisers within the government. I became a waiter in the Houses of Parliament. When I was debriefed at the end of my time there one of the officers was a Detective Superintendent Hardcastle who you knew I believe."

"Yes and did you find any?"

"Yes two MP's and a Baronet."

Renton then said "Righto we need to track down on the 1954 Recruits list Henson, Bill Smith, Campbell and Wilson and Horton. Reg Passport Office, Steve and Tina contact the police stations nearest to where they were born or their last addresses, Jack and Dennis contact Smudge Smith and your local contacts. See you all tomorrow."

David said "I have seen Inspector Walker and he is providing 4 constables so this evening we are doing house to house in Bentley and see those people we missed before."

"Excellent."

25
Bawtry

Renton arrived at the station at 9.15am checked his tray and reset the date on his calendar 29th April 1966 and then went down to the collators.

"I received another postcard from our man in Rio" he passed it to Reg.

Reg said "Yes his little joke, but God willing his arrogance will lead him back here for whatever reason and then you will have the joy of seeing him at the Old Bailey. Anything from the Chief yesterday?"

"No not a lot really just that anything we find we must share it with Special Branch."

"He must have done some time with them in his old Force."

"Well that says it all."

"How do you fancy some fresh air on this lovely morning?"

"Why."

"The passport office wouldn't tell me about Horton, some protocol getting in the way. However thanks to his massive card index the bod on the end of the line said that Horton was born in some place called Bawtry, no other details, I bet you Frank knows someone in a blue uniform in Bawtry."

"Good then once he has finished with morning prayers he can give me the tour."

Exactly one hour later Frank walked in.

"Do you know any coppers in Bawtry?" said Renton he winked at Reg

"Alfred Colman, why?"

"Because you are taking me to see Alfred apparently Horton was born in Bawtry."

Fifteen minutes later they were on their way.

"What can you tell me about Bawtry and PC Colman?"

"Mustard man behind his back for obvious reasons he has been the local bobby for donkeys. Bawtry has a pit, a library and RAF Bawtry occasionally some friction between them and the locals. It was part of Bomber Command during the war. However they didn't have a runway so they used Bircotes. The friction is because the local girls liked the RAF boys. The school, the Mayflower School is named after the original Mayflower because the Pilgrims leader was William Bradford who hailed from nearby Austerfield."

"Yes Steve mentioned something about Austerfield."

They arrived at the police station to find PC Colman washing the windows.

"Hello Alf." said Frank.

"Bugger me Detective Inspector Dipper."

"Thank you Alf this is Superintendent Renton and he is ready for a mug of black coffee and tea for me."

They went inside and Alf put the kettle on and produced a tin marked biscuits. "Shortbread straight from Bonny Scotland."

As they dunked their biscuits Frank said "What can you tell us about Gerald Horton?"

"Ah yes the Horton family the youngest is Gerry, has 2 brothers and a sister. Dad and sons worked in the pit, their actual claim is they come from a long line of poachers. Old man Horton and his brother supplied every butcher in a 10 mile radius during World War 1 and beyond. Rabbit's hares pheasants partridge and the nobility's trout. However Gerry was a disappointment to the family business because he just didn't have the nous to be a poacher, bit clumsy but a good miner, built like a bull."

"Have you seen him lately?"

"No not since he went off to do his National Service. The old man says he is a bit of a gypsy moving from pit to pit and there are quite a few to choose from. Last I heard he might be at Frickley or maybe Grimey."

"Can you describe him to us?"

Five foot eight, six feet wide all muscle no neck banned from playing rugby I mean who gets sent off for being too violent at rugby not the sharpest tool in the box."

Renton showed Alf the group photograph "Which one is Horton?"

"The lump at the extreme right."

"Is it worth talking to the family?"

"They wouldn't give us the snot of the end of their noses."

"Righto if he surfaces can you give us a call."

On the way back to the station Renton said "I think we will put Austin on the scent to Frickley and Grimethorpe. And what will the treat today be at Dick's Diner?"

"Friday will be cod chips and mushy peas for the traditionalists, for the rest sausage chips and mushy peas."

26
Austin

Renton and Frank walked out of Dick's Diner full of cod and chips. "Do you think Austin will be in the Legion for lunch now?"

Frank said "More than likely."

They went into the Legion, which had the main bar and also 2 small rooms to one side if members wanted a bit of privacy. In one of them was Austin with a pint of mild and the Yorkshire Post crosswords .Renton and Frank sat down opposite him "Another?" said Renton pointing to the mild.

"No thank you Ralph just the one for lunch."

"We need your local knowledge." said Renton "Gerald Horton formerly of Bawtry may now be working at Frickley or Grimethorpe pit can you find him?"

"You've been talking to Alf Colman."

"We need to find Horton before the killer does."

"Fine I will get back to you by 4pm if I can."With that he drained the pint and walked out of the Legion with Renton and Frank.

They parted company with Austin and Renton said "He seemed very confident considering debrief is at 4pm in 3 hours."

"Austin and Smudge have every mine and village in a 20 mile radius in their pockets."

Back at the station they went into the collators and Frank put the kettle on. Reg was typing furiously. Frank said "Do you want some water to cool that machine down Reg?"

"Funnyman I am typing up the latest ready for the briefing and then hopefully actually get to eat my lunch but a cuppa would be nice."

10 minutes later with a cuppa in one hand and a sandwich in the other Reg said "I contacted my mate in the Foreign Office again. Andrew Wilson came back to York he was a butcher by trade and emigrated to New Zealand. He served in Suez unfortunately he drowned last year. William Smith the blacksmith has never applied for a passport since coming back so no idea where he is. But David Henson applied for a passport last April, his address is in Shirebrook and his occupation is a hewer."

"A what?" said Renton

"A hewer top of the tree in miner speak as a youngster you start at the bottom which is a door trapper, also looking after the pit ponies then labourer then miner and finally a hewer who has proved he can dig that coal out no matter what thus making someone a lot richer than himself."

"Grim"

"Very" said Reg "here is his address."He handed Renton a note."He doesn't have a telephone but he is off this weekend and if the weather is good he will be either in his garden or allotment."

"Very good how do you know he will be off this weekend telepathy perhaps." said Renton

"One thing that is really efficient in a pit is the pit managers secretary's and Dolores Wrigley is efficient. There is more James Campbell came back to England in 1956 and finished his surveyors course in London. He then applied for a passport giving his occupation as surveyor and gave his address as some place in South Africa that started with two consonants. The address given is the company office for a diamond mine. All that is now typed up in the briefing file."

"Righto, I am now going to my office to see what Foxy has left me to clear up, see you at 4pm."

4pm briefing arrived. Renton read out what Reg had typed up then not seeing Austin turned to Jack "Anything from you?"

"Not a sausage but dad will be here shortly I believe he is watering the horse."

Austin walked in "Aha I see you are all waiting with bated breath. Gerald Horton worked at Grimethorpe for a while and being short of the grey matter and being endowed with too much muscle and not being happy with his deputy, he clocked him and the magistrates gave him 6 months. He then disappeared for a while possibly went to Wales is the rumour. He is apparently very good at chatting up the ladies and has no qualms about living off them in return for certain favours. He then started work at Frickley two years ago, a changed man a good worker always on time and not picking fights with anyone. Two months ago he said he had come into some money from an inheritance and stopped working. Last seen two weeks ago in the Chequers with a woman which isn't unusual and was flash with his money not sure where he is actually living but I am working on that."

"Righto thanks for that Austin. Reg I need you to find out what Campbell did after South Africa, a hard ask I know. Also what about William Smith the blacksmith according to the list he went to Suez. Steve you and I will be going to Shirebrook tomorrow, I will pick you up at yours at 9.30am.

27
Shirebrook

Renton picked up Steve at 9.30am and said "What are we doing working on a Saturday when we could be lazing around like the others."

"Apart from Reg, who will be in the office overhauling his cards for the hundredth time."

"According to Reg Shirebrook pit was sunk at the end of the last century." said Renton, he continued "It became a very prosperous pit connected underground to another pit Pleasley. Also at the same time a model village was created of 500 houses for the miners and their families."

"Is there a bakery on the way sir?"

"I bet there is and for your cheek you can buy the rolls and coffee."

On the way into Shirebrook there was a bakery and 10 minutes later Steve returned to the car with hot bacon rolls and coffees. Having eaten their rolls Renton drove to the Police Station where he spoke to Sergeant Moston who had been forewarned by Reg. Back in the car Renton said "Very helpful, here is a rough map with the allotments nearest to Henson's address."

Steve said "What is the lure of sitting here amongst a lot of tumbledown huts and what looks like a wasteland to me."

"Ah yes the joy of getting away from the wife, peace and quiet and fresh air something you do not get working a mile underground. You will turn to an allotment as salvation from the wife and 6 kids one day." There was a man near the gate sitting on a barrel cleaning the dirt off some carrots.

"Can you help us find David Henson?" Renton said as he showed the man his ID card.

"That's me."

"We would like to ask you about your time when you were doing National Service."

"Aye, follow me." He walked to a shed and pulled out a couple of old chairs when they were seated Steve took out the group photograph with Kowalski in it,

Renton said "This photograph we think was taken in Berlin about 1955 can you tell us who is who."

"I don't know the tall bloke in the middle but the one on the left down at his feet is Eric Cooper, then Stewart the tall man no idea then bully Carlyle and then meathead Gerry Horton. What's this all about?"

Renton then told him about the deaths in Doncaster "It is imperative we track down Horton and Carlyle."

"I have not see Horton since National Service but Carlyle I saw let me think last April in London. My nephew was trying out for Spurs so a group of us went to London and made a weekend of it. After his try out we went to see Big Ben and then went to a pub somewhere near, I cannot remember the name. Carlyle was in there talking to some bloke. They were both well dressed. The other bloke had that look of an accountant, had a briefcase, bit like yours. I avoided him."

"You haven't seen him since?"

"No I didn't like him or the others. Horton wasn't too bad as long as he hadn't been drinking, but Carlyle and his two minions Cooper and Stewart were poison. I kept away from them. Suez wasn't particularly pleasant but it would have been hell with them there. How did you find me?"

"Through your passport application, going anywhere nice?"

"Australia to live, I am a carpenter by trade, the wife and me having been saving for a while, get away from the small minds around here and the pit."

"I wish you well. Oh by the way do you know what happened to Bill Smith the blacksmith after National Service?"

"Bill grand lad he ended up working as a blacksmith in a pit in Kent but his wife's mum died and left them quite a bit of money and he now has his own blacksmithing forge in the Midlands somewhere doing very well apparently."

Back in the car Renton said "Drive into Shirebrook let's find a phonebox, I think I will ring Reg."

They stopped at a telephone kiosk and Renton went in. He came out and got in the car." Horton's been found, dead on a farm at South Elmsall, throat slit. Head for Doncaster through Blyth, Reg has given me directions to the farm."

They drove through Hooton Pagnell and then into the village, heading for the pit. Then along a country lane as they approached the farm they could see Sergeant Smudge Smith standing by his motorcycle. They shook hands.

"The body has gone to the mortuary. Your fingerprint chap is very keen I am pleased to say. Follow me."

They crossed the road away from the farm buildings to a haystack but made up of bales of hay. Round the back there was a slight recess in the haystack with the ground covered in blood.

Smudge said "The body was propped up in a sitting position leaning against yon stack. He had had a knock on the back of his head and as you can see from the blood killed here. The farmer Mr. King says this area is used by couples for a bit of slap and tickle. Horton died late last night, Mr King checked this area at 8pm last night and has given a statement to that effect. I gave it to your young fingerprint lad. The farmer found the body about 9am this morning. The Doc came and certified death and he reckons that the killer knocked him on the head to stun him then tied him up then gave him the wire treatment round his neck."

"Righto Smudge thanks for that."

28
Blackmail

They returned to the station, by this time it was just 1.30pm. In the collators was Frank with Reg "Just in time for a drink" said Reg.

Sitting down with their drinks Renton said "That farmhouse looks quite medieval with those slits for windows."

Reg said "Kings farm was used by the Cavaliers to get away to the North from the Roundheads. They met in Hooton Pagnell. There is apparently a tunnel from there to the farm where there would be fresh horses waiting for them to escape Cromwell's men. Here is the statement from Mr King, it says he found the body about 9am after he fed the pigs which he always did from 8.30am onwards. Here is Horton's wallet."He handed Renton an evidence bag "85 smackers in it so not robbery."

Frank said "As there is nothing in the wallet to say where Horton lived Jack and Austin have gone to Elmsall to see if they can find where he lived."

Just then his telephone rang, Reg answered it then said "Leslie Reid is in the front office and wants to see the boss in private."

Renton went down to the front office to find an agitated Leslie Reid, he took him into the interview room. He asked the office PC to bring a cup of tea.

"Oh I am in a bit of a state Mr Renton, I don't know if I should tell you." said Reid.

Renton said "Just take a few breaths and relax you are not under any pressure." Just then the cup of tea arrived and after a couple of sips Renton said "Now what is concerning you?"

"I loved Harold and he was always very kind to me not like some of the ignorant folk around here. Sometimes when he had a glass of wine too much he would confide in me about his past. He dearly love his ma and pa and about escaping from those horrible Nazi men, of course they had to his ma was a Jewish lady. He also loved his time in the army. Good times and some bad, He had to leave Germany because certain nasty people had been threatening him and others trying to blackmail him for large sums of money."

"Did he tell you the names of these people?"

"Not at first."

"Not at first." said Renton "So how long had this been going on?"

"Two years, Harold was a generous person I mean all that food he cooked for the pensioners he paid out of his own pocket and he lent some money to Gerry."

"Was that Gerry Horton?"

"I only knew him as Gerry, good looking man very muscular and quite polite not like the others."

"The others?"

"Oh yes I would call Harold St. Jude the patron saint of lost causes."

"So who were the others then Leslie?"

"Well there was Terry he lent him £250 for his sister."

"Do you mean Elsie Stewart?"

Reid leaned forward and whispered "Well yes, she had a drink problem and he wanted to get her in a clinic in Leeds and it would take that money to get her on the straight and narrow."

"Do you think that was a loan or was Stewart blackmailing Harold?"

"Oh my goodness I am a naïve fellow perhaps it was blackmail he was a vulgar man every other word was a swear word."

"The money that Harold gave to Gerry was that a loan?"

"Oh yes I think so they were good friends."

"Do you think they were as close as you and Harold were."

"Yes they had slept together and Gerry was a bit of a looker."

"Anyone else you can remember who Harold might have lent money to?"

Reid hesitated and then whispering again he said "There was one who came I don't know is name exactly but Harold called him Dekko. He came to the house and he was quite arrogant towards me. They went in the kitchen and I heard him say "Is that one of your nancy boys then Pole."

"Do you know where this Dekko was from was he English or German?"

"English well that night we had a few drinks and I said that he seemed quite an arrogant man. Harold said that he could be like that. He said that normally he met him in Bradford where he lived."

"Do you know the name Eric Cooper?"

"Eric oh yes he was known in every pub this side of the Pennines I saw what happened to him in the newspaper."

"Do you know if Harold knew him or mentioned him in your talks?"

"No he never mentioned him."

"Well thank you Leslie for coming in and I hope you feel better and if you think of anything please feel free to pop in."

Renton then showed him out and returned to the collators.

29
Horton

Frank said "While you was talking to Leslie Reid Jack rang they have found where Horton lived but not a lot to see. They are on their way back via his mum who has baked us some scones."

Reg said "I think someone has been helping themselves to the cash in our tea fund. Two weeks ago there was a pound missing and today there is another pound missing. So from now on the kitty will be locked in the exhibit locker."

Steve said "Do you think it is worth fingerprinting the tin?"

Renton said "No we won't go down that street, we will go with Reg's suggestion. I have the spare key for the locker and if I should ever get a day off I will pass it to Frank or you Steve, whoever is on duty."

Reg said "When I took over from Fred Harmon he was fond of saying there are nearly as many villains in the force as out on the street."

Frank said "Fred was an ex tankie in the war and he hated the words brewing up because when a tank was hit and burning they called it brewing up. Not a nice way to die."

Austin and Jack walked in carrying a large cake tin Austin said "Can I smell a kettle on then?"

Frank reached out for the tin.

"Aha hands off, tea first and then you can have a cheese scone." said Austin.

15 minutes later and all parties duly refreshed Jack said."Horton rented a room in a house round the back of the fire station, some sort of granny flat. £25 a month including your laundry but not food. He had his own front door a room come bedroom and a bathroom with

toilet. Looking in the dustbin his idea of meals was pork pies, tins of bully beef, fruit and raw onion and lots of milk. Under the bed was a small box with a wallet and containing £75 and a school exercise book with names and addresses. Women are written in red, men in black not sure what that was about. Couple pairs of mining overalls, shirts and underwear, that's about it. The exercise book and the money is in this bag." Jack put the bag on the table.

Renton said "From my chat with Reid it seems that Horton slept with Harold and borrowed money from him but it seemed a convivial arrangement, whereas Stewart borrowed £250 from Harold and maybe blackmailed him. Jack and Austin have done a summary on Horton so over to you Jack."

"Gerald Horton born 21st June 1934 in Bawtry, a family of miners and known for poaching. Not known for his academic ability but as strong as a bull went down the pit at 15. Then National Service and demobbed. Bit of a gap then worked at Grimethorpe then at Frickley. Left a couple of weeks ago said he had come into an inheritance but perhaps the money came from his lover. Found dead this morning at Kings Farm, Broad Lane, South Elmsall behind a haystack. Smudge Smith rang here and we cranked it up with Doctor Wells in attendance and Peter. Over to Peter."

Peter said "Doctor Wells certified death and said he would drop the certificate in with his post mortem report. Horton had blood on the back of his head and with his short hair you could see the dent in his skull. So Doctor Wells reckons the killer stunned Horton so he could tie up his hands and feet so he couldn't fight back but the Doc thinks he was maybe unconscious when he gave him the wire treatment, I took the usual photographs and once they have dried I will drop them in to you."

Austin said "We saw Smudge and he said that Horton was attractive to men and women preferably married women and that's why he was kicked out of a lot of pubs for fending off the husbands."

Reg said "So tied and wired like a turkey and it's not even Christmas."

Renton said "Reid said that Carlyle had been to see Harold and perhaps we can presume he was blackmailing him about all the stuff they did in Berlin. Now I am duty officer tomorrow and it is the weekend so I want you to concentrate on Sandall Wood split your shifts to take in the whole of the day and evening. Reid also said that he thought Carlyle lived in Bradford so we will go that way next week. Reg will contact their collator and see if he has anything local on Carlyle. So I will be in the Red Lion at 6pm usual rules, anyone else?"

Tina put her hand up "We finished the house to house and the house opposite Crowley's belongs to a Walter Gregory who we are told is a massive curtain twitcher and has lived there the longest so knows what goes on. He is away at his sister's so we put a note through the door to contact us as soon as he can."

"Excellent." Renton said "See you in the pub."

They all stood up and Peter said "Can I say something?"They all groaned and sat down.

"When Sergeant Ramsden went to Scotland Yard he came back with his mates telephone number in their fingerprint bureau and said to ring anytime. So I did and asked him about the fingerprint on the padlock from the hut in Sandall Beat Wood. He said that they had no trace of it in their files. I said would there have been a record of all the people who had done National Service and he said there would have been the problem was finding the files. He said could I narrow it down for him so I gave him the names of all those that served in 1954 from the North of England effectively all the ones on the list we have of those that joined with Duggan. He rang me this morning and said that although the fingerprint on its own cannot be used in court it could be used to trace the person."

Frank said "Come on Peter I am wetting myself in anticipation?"

"It belongs to James Campbell."

There was stunned silence then Frank said "Bugger me only a couple on that list we cannot trace and he is one of them."

"That's worth more than one pint at 6pm." said Renton.

30
Oscar Peplinski

It was 10am on a sunny Sunday morning in the collators Reg was talking to Renton as Frank returned from morning prayers.

"The first day of May, hikers day and the sun is shining." said Reg.

"Hikers day."said Renton

Reg said "Yes traditionally the first of May is the start of the hiking season. The Ramblers fought long and hard to have the right to ramble so no doubt with this weather the Dales will be bursting at the seams."

Austin walked in and said "Do I smell a kettle on and where are my wife's cheese scones?"

Reg produced the cake tin from a drawer "And there are 5 left."

"What a bombshell from Peter yesterday," said Frank "Campbell as the murderer of Stewart and Cooper at least, maybe even Crowley."

"I think so." said a deep voice from the corridor. In walked a man 6 foot 4 inches tall, wide shouldered with a full black beard, wearing a suit.

"Hello I am Oskar Peplinski, mind if I have a cup of tea, black no sugar and here is ten shillings for you tea fund. He shook their hands, except for Austin who said "We have already met."

"How's that?" said Frank.

Oskar said "I needed some lodgings while I am working here and my uncle put me in touch with Austin."

Austin said "Bob and I were in Passchendaele with the Marines."

Oskar said "I was told not to mention the mud."

Frank said to him "So you think Campbell is our man for the killings?"

"Yes for Cooper and Stewart but I am not so sure for Crowley."

Austin said "Come on lad put them out of their misery."

"The army list you have shows Campbell in training and in Germany which he was, but he was recruited to go undercover in Berlin. There had been suspicions about Crowley and when he arrived I was already there undercover. I knew about him but he didn't know about me. By the time he went into training with the others he had already been trained for the undercover role, on your list he appears to have been born in 1934 but he was two years older than the rest. He had a degree, educated at a private school and spoke several languages especially French and very fluent in German. Alistair Duggan confided in both of us separately about his suspicions of Kowalski. Stewart was passing low level stuff to Carlyle and Cooper who was working in the orderly office was looking through various despatches and passing that to Carlyle. There reward was boozing and whoring at the Iguana with both sexes when their two years were up Cooper and Stewart returned to Yorkshire same for Horton. Carlyle had been driving the brass around and had established contact through Kowalski to a Russian agent. He disappeared from Berlin but the Russians were training him with a view to using him in London. Kowalski skipped from Berlin ending up as Harold Crowley in Yorkshire. Carlyle was on a good number with Crowley and making a lot of money but when Kowalski skipped I think he had found out through his contact that the Russians were planning to use Carlyle to kill him. It's possible that perhaps the West ie the Yanks, French and British powers that be were going to find out what was going on and maybe show the Russians up internationally not very good for detente. Despite the press over here showing the Russians and the rest of the world at loggerheads there was a lot going on between them and us."

Renton said "So what happened to Carlyle is he working for the Russians and killing Cooper, Stewart and Kowalski and recently Horton as part of some contract?"

"Carlyle vanished so we thought either the Russians had him killed or they were using him as an assassin." Said Peplinski.

Renton said "So what do you know about Carlyle that we don't?"

"Born in Lincoln, his family were originally from London, but his grandfather was from somewhere in Russia very close to the Polish Border, near Minsk we think. Somehow the family made it to the East End of London where Carlyle's father was born. I think Campbell is now on a revenge mission against Carlyle and his toadies because he and Duggan were cousins but only Campbell knew that."

Renton said "I think we should have an open mind about who killed who. Both Carlyle and Campbell have a motive for killing Cooper and the rest and also Crowley. Carlyle because he is covering his back by getting rid of his past and Campbell for what they did to young Duggan. Maybe they are working together. The only link we have at the moment is that print on the padlock."

"Different change in the MO because Cooper, Stewart and Horton were all killed in the open, whereas Crowley was killed in his bed, quite different. However if he never went out how could you do the job." said Peplinski.

Renton said "I presume Austin told you about Horton?"

"Yes."

Frank said "What do you know about the Vlad character?"

"Vladimir had many surnames including Sokolov and Sokolo is falcon in English and falcon was his codename. He found out that his Russian masters were going to have him eliminated. So he and Kowalski were lovers and he warned him that maybe the Russians were going to have a cleaning out session. Several East German agents had already been bumped off. Perhaps Kowalski was next."

Renton said "We found diamonds and cash at Crowley's address."

Peplinksi said "The Russians always paid their agents in diamonds or gold, both are the currency of the world. Diamonds except to an expert are untraceable, roubles and Deutschmarks could be traced. Kowalski sold quite a few diamonds into dollars and sterling. He had a jeweller in Berlin he used. It's quite possible he was wiring money to an account somewhere in Britain. Vlad went on the run dodging Russians on his way to London where he turned himself in to one of the M services. He then passed on info on Kowalski who then adopted the name of Crowley and also passed on info on Carlyle and what was happening at the then perimeter now the Berlin Wall."

"So what can you tell us about Campbell what sort of man is he?"

"Highly intelligent and totally ruthless. I watched him interrogate a Russian, it's amazing what you can do with a heated spoon. His father is a big cheese in South Africa. He went out there to help him but ended up hanging around with the security guards most of them ex Foreign Legion, mercenaries that sort of thing. He disappeared with some of daddies cash. Seen by special forces in Africa in the Foreign Legion. Then we think he went freelance."

"So you have no idea where Carlyle is now?" said Renton

"Nope, since I have been in the civvy police all my contacts are either dead or disappeared from sight. Dropped out to survive maybe." said Peplinski.

Renton said "I will ring Duggan senior now and tomorrow Oskar and I will go and see him and we will find out more about his connection with the Campbells. We will see you all on Tuesday. You can all knock off now and Reg please go home."

31
Deuteronomy

Renton picked up Oskar from Austin's in Warmsworth a suburb of Doncaster at 9am.

"How are the lodgings?" said Renton

"Yes very good, mother's cooking and we have come to an arrangement I don't pay rent but I am digging the vegetable plot in the back garden and then starting on the allotment."

"Very into self sufficiency is Austin and best of luck he has 2 allotment plots. Did you get a chance to look over Reg's summary of where we are so far.

"Yes, first murder victim found on 13th April and here we are nearly 3 weeks on and a total of 4 victims. But with a possible suspect so not bad going I think. So why are we going to see Duggan senior. I see he was a Para in the war and got the MC."

"Yes that is correct. Initially we thought perhaps being in a wheelchair was a cover and he and his son Alexander were out for revenge. So we put an officer out undercover to see the lie of the land. Senior is partially paralysed and son Alexander runs the farm. We will be stopping in Bawtry at a bakers I know and you can go and buy a nice cake to accompany a cuppa."

"Softening them up?"

"Oh come on you are ex-army it's called a Hearts and Minds campaign."

40 minutes later they arrived at the farm and presented Helen Duggan with fruit cake. Renton introduced Oskar to the family 10 minutes later they were all sitting on the patio with a slice of cake and a drink.

Renton said "I hope Chief Superintendent Bullstone has given you some enlightenment on your son's death?"

"Yes it was very informative." said Mr Duggan.

"Then perhaps you can offer us some enlightenment about a certain James Campbell?" said Renton.

"Why do you want to know about James." said Alexander.

Renton produced the list of the recruits who had been at Catterick and gave it to Mr Duggan and said "As you can see from the ticks we have managed to trace all but a couple William Smith who was or is a blacksmith Derek Carlyle and James Campbell who we have been told is related to your family. So it's possible that one of those three could be the killer. Also for your information Kowalski has been living in Bentley a suburb of Doncaster under the name of Harold Crowley he has also been killed in the same way as Cooper and Stewart and also Gerald Horton who you can see is eighth on the list."

Duggan said "The bastard who's rifle Alistair tried to clear."

"So what is the link between James Campbell and your family?"

Mr Duggan said "My wife came from a poor background. After she was born along came a second daughter Margaret and the family gave her up for adoption. A couple in Edinburgh adopted her and kept the name Margaret. They gave her a lot of love and an excellent education, she was a clever girl but a rebel I think now the term is wild child by the time she was 16 she was pregnant. She married the father of her child Iain Campbell, he was 22 and a qualified engineer. He came from a wealthy family. They were living in Lincoln when James was born. Iain was working on some project near Lincoln very hush hush. But one year later he was sent by his company to South Africa. He ended up running the company which was into diamond mines. When James was 7 his father sent him to a boarding school by 13 a private tutor in Edinburgh. By this time Margaret had moved back to Edinburgh. When he was 18 he went to university where he got a first in geology and engineering. Somewhere from there to National Service he underwent training to be undercover agent along came National Service which he did to get to know the others on that list he then. While in Berlin he went absent without leave so he could disappear and go undercover. He was very fluent in German and I think he relished the danger that work brought. After that he went back to South Africa but there was some friction between him and Iain and he went a bit wild and disappeared."

Renton said "So when did James find out that Alistair was his cousin?"

"About 2 weeks after Alistair had died. He had written to his father who then flew to Germany for a brief visit and saw him there."

Duggan turned to his son and said "Alex can you bring the family box?"

Alex went upstairs and returned with a polished wooden box which he handed to his dad. Duggan opened it and took out a letter and gave it to Renton. He read it and then passed it to Oskar.

Renton said "It's very brief and the postscript has VIMSTL what's that all about."

Duggan said "It stands for Vengeance is mine sayeth the Lord. It is from Deuteronomy in the bible."

Oskar said "The letter is very brief and is basically a bereavement thing but I think the word vengeance is really what it is all about."

Duggan said "Yes I know what you are saying but at the time I just thought it was his frustration at not being able to help Alistair and maybe somehow prevent it. James was like his father very driven and he needed to prove himself hence doing two degrees at the same time. No grey areas just like his father."

Renton said "We now know that when James left South Africa he enlisted in the Foreign Legion and Cooper and Stewart were killed with a technique that had been used by the Legionaire's. Have you had any communication with him since that letter. Do you have a photograph of him at all?"

"We haven't heard from him since then."He took a framed photograph out of the box and handed it to Renton.

"Do you have another not framed that we can use?"

Duggan handed him a photograph with all their names written on the back.

Renton said "Can I have this so we can copy it and then I will send you this one back."

"Keep it. As you can see Alistair has his single stripe on his uniform. This was taken just before they were posted abroad."

"Righto." said Renton "Up until we found out that James was related to Alistair we thought the killer might be Derek Carlyle and by killer our victims we assumed he was covering his tracks from the past. I am sure I don't have to tell you that if James contacts you, you must let us know, also if Carlyle appears same thing."

"And charge them." said Duggan.

Oskar said "But that word vengeance does smack of revenge."

Duggan said "Yes I know what you mean." He then struggled out of his chair and said to Oskar "I would like to thank you for what you did for Alistair and James in Berlin, I know now from Bullstone that you kept an eye on them." he extended his hand. They shook hands.

Oskar said "The comradeship of the army."

They drove away and then stopped and Renton said "Look at this photograph an unsmiling Carlyle because he hasn't got the stripe,

Cooper on one side, Horton on the other and Stewart behind like his bodyguards."

Once back at the station Renton went upstairs to see Peter and ask if he could print off several photographs of Carlyle and Campbell from the group photograph from Duggan.

"Yes boss no sweat and I will enlarge them slightly."

32
Debrief no.4

It was 4pm as Renton went into the collators to find Peter talking to Reg.

"Here is the original photograph, I am still developing the copy but will have it and the single copies ready for tomorrow."

The others arrived and made themselves a drink, they then settled down.

"Righto everyone I would like to introduce DS Oskar spelt with a k Peplinski, he is now helping us with the murders. We are now on day 19 and we have four murder victims. I think due to the way Cooper, Stewart and Horton were murdered then we can probably say that their killer was James Campbell. Thanks to the fingerprint on the padlock and that the technique used was used by the Foreign Legion and Campbell was one of their own. This morning Oskar and I went to see the Duggan family."

Renton then told them about the conversation and the letter from Campbell. "We know Campbell has a vehicle did he kill Cooper and then transport him to the butter cross. I don't think so I think they met there and that's where he did it looking at the amount of blood in situ."

Frank said "Taking a risk doing it in such a public place and let's not forget the drunken witness that saw a man standing next to a white Commer style van,"

"Yes perhaps that's part of the kick who knows any thoughts about where Horton was killed was he lured there on the promise of sex. We know he liked a bit of both. Thoughts about Crowley's death."

Jack said "Crowley preferred men, Horton liked both Cooper had previous for meeting men in public toilets and Stewart was never seen with a woman or come to that a man. But they all liked what they got at this club in Berlin. I think Carlyle was blackmailing

Crowley possibly about his sexuality, the people in pit villages are not the most tolerant of queers or was Carlyle blackmailing him about his past in German and threatening to let the authorities know where he was. Crowley did a runner and left Carlyle to fend for himself. For what Crowley got up to in Germany it would be prison for him for sure."

Frank said "Let us not forget Malcom Mobley."

"Who the hell is Malcolm Mobley?" said Renton.

"Malcolm Mobley was the only conchie in South Elmsall, he was artistic bit of a painter and went to prison for his views. However he agreed to be a stretcher bearer providing he didn't have to carry a rifle. Wounded 3 times his brother had enlisted and he was killed in August 1918. Malcolm came home and got a job in the council offices. He was constantly teased about being a fairy by the two-faced parochial people of a mining village. So he hung himself. So I think that's why Crowley kept quiet about his sexuality."

"Righto here is a photograph of the recruits after training and knowing they were going to be posted abroad. You can see that Alastair Duggan has got his one stripe up. Carlyle surrounded by his rats is not happy Peter is going to do us some single copies of Carlyle and Campbell so that you can carry them with you when out and about. I also have Doc Wells post mortem report on Horton. He was clubbed from the back doc thinks to render him immobile so he could tie him up and then kill him. The dent in his skull is perfectly round and the Doc says that the only club that would leave this is a knobkerrie which was used by the Zulus in Africa Oskar over to you."

Oskar said "Carlyle's grandparents were from Russia and came to London When I was working undercover and got to know him he said his father was a carpenter and his company sent him to Lincoln where he would be working for at least a year. His wife who was heavily pregnant with Carlyle came along and they lived in a flat rented by the company. Carlyle was born in Lincoln. When the job was finished they went back to London and moved in with Grandma and Grandad who lived in Crystal Palace."

"Righto, Reg contact your records man and see if you can trace Mr and Mrs Carlyle with son Derek."

Oskar said "Francis and Evelyn Carlyle."

"Righto once we have established an address we well get Bullstones boys or maybe our old friend DS Jackson to keep tabs on it. Let's call it a day and see you all in the Red Lion 6pm usual drill. One more thing Reg can you find a blacksmith working near Newark. Alex Duggan mentioned it when we said about William Smith?"

Frank said "Bit of a coincidence that Campbell and Carlyle were both born in Lincoln."

Austin explained to Oskar about the wallet and the Red Lion.

33
Inkerman

Renton arrived at his desk at 8.30am, he looked at his calendar Tuesday 3rd May 1966 as he sat down he thought 3 weeks since the first murder and although he had one or two suspects he didn't know whether they were in this country or not. He then saw in his tray a note it was from Frank "The Chief would like to see you after morning prayers when Benson has gone say 11am."

Also in his tray were 2 files for him to go through and mark up for court excellent he thought these will keep him occupied away from Benson. One hour later he could hear Frank talking to Benson as he escorted him upstairs to the Chief's office. Just before 11am and the files sorted his telephone rang and a whispered voice said "All clear."

Renton went into the Chief's office and sat down. The Chief asked him about the progress of the murder enquiry. Renton explained where they were. The chief then said "I had Benson in here this morning at prayers and he told me that he is standing down as chairman of the Watch Committee and the person who has been elected in his place is George Maynard an excellent chap and the cousin of our own Ted Maynard. So that's about it for now Ralph so I will let you go to your troops."

Renton said "I thought Henry Sykes was going to be the chairman?"

"Yes so did I but apparently Henry is quite happy being vice chairmen and that is good for us with the top two being so helpful and communicative."

Renton went down to the collators to hear Frank telling them about Benson.

"Here boss have you heard the good news?" said Reg.

"Yes" said Renton "The Chief has just told me with great relief and his replacement is Ted's cousin George Maynard. Now give me some more good news about Campbell or Carlyle."

Reg said "I rang the Records Office and I asked for an address for Francis and Evelyn preferably London also Lincoln and they will ring me back."

Oskar arrived, made a black tea and sat down.

Renton said "So what would the gang of four get in the way of rewards for their treason against our soldiers and country."

"Remember their pay was pretty rubbish and they were all young so sex was readily available on the street let alone in a nightclub where Crowley was the part owner. Sex in a mining village was convincing some young woman that you were a God in the sack. The Blue Iguana was a club, pub and brothel so whatever you wanted was there on offer, so I would think they would be paid that way. Cooper worked in the orderly office so he was checking out the despatches and I know that Stewart and Horton were getting young impressionable young soldiers drunk and finding out what they were up to. As their two years progressed Carlyle was getting in with Crowley and they were drugging certain officers and using blackmail to get the info they wanted for the Soviets."

The telephone rang and Reg answered it after a short conversation and Reg jotting down some notes he hung up and said "Records office did a sweep on the two spellings of Carlyle and found Frank and Eve Carlyle living in Maitland Road in Crystal Palace. The houses don't have obvious numbers but have names such as Montgomery or Wakefield but they live at Inkerman so over to Captain Bullshit and his Special Bods."

"Ooh dear" said Frank don't you mean Chief Superintendent Bullstone of the estimable Special Branch."

"Whatever." said Reg. "I have contacted Bradford to see if they have anything local on Carlyle."

Renton said "Righto I will give Bullstone a call and ask him to set his dogs on Inkerman. Peter came down earlier and here are the photographs of Carlyle and Campbell. Steve and Tina to Bradford pop in to Bradford Central and let them know you are in town just making some general enquiries I will ring their Superintendent and let him know, Jack and Dennis same here in Doncaster and Oskar and Austin off to South Elmsall. Austin to introduce Oskar to Smudge and his boys Reg you might get a call from my chum in the Foreign Office if they have found out if Campbell and Carlyle are in this country. See you all back here tomorrow morning with some excellent results............I hope."

34
Lincoln

Renton arrived at his usual time of 8.30am and checked his tray a couple more files for his attention. He decided a mug of hot black coffee was more important and went to the collators.

Reg said "Your contact rang yesterday afternoon. As far as they know Carlyle is still in the country, the last address he gave was Inkerman and the time before when he was out of the country was an address in Winchester which doesn't exist. As for Campbell he has been in the country for about 6 months, came from France. Gave an address in London which turns out to be a florist with no accommodation."

"Austin said "Oskar has met the irrepressible Smudge we gave him the two mug shots and he will be briefing his boys and told him that Campbell has a set of wheels.

Jack said "We went to the market and Dennis knows most of the stallholders most of them went to school with him so over to you Dennis."

"When the market closes some of the stallholders go for a beer. My cousin Ellen has had a stall for donkeys years and she and some of the women go to the Mason's Arms we gave her the mug shots and she is going to show them to the others next market day and ask around if they get anything they will ring Reg.

Steve said "We went to Bradford via Wakefield and the collator has a new photocopier so took a few copies which he will send to Bradford, not a lot happening there so we went to Lincoln. Tina went into a florist and on the notice board was a cutting out of a newspaper with the name Carlyle Carpenters on it. The lady in there said that it had been on the board quite a few years."

Tina said "We went to the market and passed the mug shots around and one of the ladies recognised Carlyle. She said that she saw him talking to one of the stallholders on the day before St. Patricks Day, so that was a Wednesday. Carlyle with another man bit of a looker built like a brick shithouse her words but hasn't seen them since. She said that Carlyle was wearing a suit looking a bit posh and had a big roll of cash."

"What about their demeanour?"said Renton

"They seemed fine very chatty."

"Righto so write up your reports and see you all tomorrow."

Just then in walked Doctor Wells and said "May I just give you a brief resume about the death of Gerald Horton." He handed the report to Renton. "As I was saying Gerald Horton was killed sometime near midnight possibly shall we say about one hour afterwards. He was bashed on the back of his head with a very powerful blow using a club with a ball like end now the only item I can think like this is a knobkerrie used by various tribesmen in Africa, there is a similar type of club also was used by the Indians in America. Having rendered Horton unconscious he then tied him up so as to render him unable to fight back. I am told he had a reputation as a brawler. He was then garrotted with the double wire like Cooper and Stewart, very professional unlike the attack on Crowley which was very messy. So I must dash cheerio for now."

Renton made another coffee and said to Frank "The Chief is getting pressure from the Attorney General why we haven't arrested anyone and did we need some help from the Mets. He assured him that we had not got to that stage just yet."

35
Walter Gregory

Renton had arrived at the office at his usual time, glanced through a couple of files and then went down to the collators he made himself and Reg a drink and as they were chatting the telephone rang. Reg answered it and said "There is an old boy in the front office a Walter Gregory, he lives opposite Howell and has been away. He has found a note amongst his mail asking him to contact Doncaster Police."

Steve said "We dropped slips in the houses that didn't answer when we did the house to house enquiries only about three I think certainly in that street."

Renton and Steve went to the front office and were introduced to Walter Gregory by the duty constable. They then showed him into the interview room.

"Would you like a cup of tea Mr Gregory?" said Renton

"Nay lad but a glass of council pop wunt go amiss."

Once the glass of water had arrived Renton explained about the death of Crowley and said "Do you mind if my colleague makes some notes?"

"Nay lad fire away."

Walter said "I have been told Harold was killed in his bed?"

Renton ignored the question and said "Did you know Harold very well Walter?"

"Oh aye grand fellah. I helped with the cooking at the Institute I was a cook in the war, Army Catering Corps, got scars and t'medal to prove it."

"So just you two did all the cooking for all those pensioners?"

"Oh no there was Doris she were a dinner lady and her daughter Marilyn. We did all the preparation and Harold would be in charge of the actual cooking. Then we would all help to serve up the food to the old folk."

"Walter can I ask how old you are?"

"Aye lad 75 this year."

"So you were 45 years old in the war."

"Haha nay lad I meant fust war the big 'un up agen the Kaiser.."

"Oh sorry about that you look younger than 75 if you don't mind me saying so." said Renton

"Very nice of you, young man, but I keep fit by doin'a bit of gardening for a couple of widows if you know what I mean."He gave an obvious wink to Renton.

"So when was the last time you saw Harold?"

"It had to be Easter Sunday. You see we cooked Good Friday and Easter Sunday for old 'uns. You know Harold paid for alt food out of his own pocket and we did a 3 course meal. A fruit juice then chicken and vegetable stew followed by sticky toffee pudding and custard. He were a grand fellah. He will be sadly missed by the old folk an I can't see the council stumpin' up for food. So we washed up on Sunday and he produced a bottle of whisky for us all to have a nip. I then went to my sisters in Middlesborough she hasn't been herself lately. Her husband died five year ago and she has never got ovver it so I go and help out wi' cooking and whatnot."

"Did Harold have regular visitors?"

Walter winked again and said "Aye Leslie popped in now and then and that was daytime and he had visitors some nights."

"In cars or vans?"

"Aye a Commer like what Bernie Hopwood has. He comes to allotment takes away all rotten vegetables for his pigs Bernie's is black but this one was white bit odd they are most colours but not white. It had some writing on the side that had been painted over and a ladder on the roof. I thought mebbe painters or summat."

"Could you see the writing?"

"Well it was summat carpentry."

"Can you say what the other word was?"

"Ooh I think mebbe Carlton I could see Car then not sure."

"Did you ever see the driver?"

"No because he always parked ont wrong side you no with driver's door facing Harold's front door."

"Did you ever ask him about his visitors when you were together in the Miners Institute?"

"Well when I first got to know him he said he had been a sergeant cook in the second war and stayed on and ended up cooking for army lad's and lasses in Germany. You could see that when we were int Institute we cooked 47 on the Friday and 52 ont Sunday. You could see he had been the boss. He said they were mates from that time."

"Did you ever go in his house?"

"Oh aye he had a party for us on New Year's Eve, it were grand fancy Indian food them little triangular cakes with vegetable and lamb inside and hot curry and rice. Doris and her husband came along wi Marilyn, Leslie, his auntie the nosey neighbour from next door bless her and a friend of mine Winnie. After the meal and some drinks he produced this German drink peach brandy, bloody hell it blew your hair off. When the others had left and it were just me and Leslie he told us about some of the army brass he hobnobbed with."

"You are sure the last time you saw him was on the Sunday at Easter?"

"Well come to think of it he came into my house with a bottle of that rocket fuel, he seemed a bit out of sorts. We had a few snifters. He said that he might have to go away for a few weeks to clear up some business and he said he would give me a key to keep an eye ont house and take in his mail. He and Leslie went away for weekends but this sounded like longer than that. But I cannot remember exactly when it might have been before Easter."

Renton then showed him the group photograph from Catterick.

"Anyone on here you recognise Walter this is very important and Harold's killer might be on here"

Walter put on his spectacles and had a good look at the faces."Aye this one here." he pointed to Cooper. "He were the lad at Hooton Pagnell I saw him in the Post. Now this one here." He pointed to Carlyle "I saw him and Harold outside the house when the Commer was there. At first I thought they were arguing, but Harold laughed at something. I were coming from the chippy and as I walked towards my house I could see the other fellah watching me as he talked to Harold it was unnerving I didn't like the look of him."

"Can you remember when this was?"

"Well it must have been in March let me see Harold had given me a half bottle of rum because it was my birthday which is 5th March so about then."

"Did you see the man or the Commer van before or after the date you have just mentioned?"

"No."

"Thank you Walter that has been most informative if you think of anything else please call me. Would you like a lift home?"

"Oh no lad a bit of shopping in Donny and then a bus home."

36
Carlton or Carlyle

Renton and Steve returned to the collators office to find the others waiting for them.

"Coffee first" said Renton He then related the conversation they had just had with Walter Gregory. "He was quite positive about it being a white Commer van."

Frank said "So we need to find that van and you say Walter thought it could be Carlton followed by Carpentry not a million miles away from Carlyle Carpentry. So he could be down here or in London."

"And to that end." said Reg "I have had a telephone call from our old friend DS Alan Jackson who is running the operation on Inkerman."

"Righto." said Renton "Steve Tina Dennis and Jack off to Lincoln. We need to know if Carlyle or Campbell have surfaced at all."

Reg said "Where is Oskar?"

Frank said "Military funeral and wake in London, five days leave."

Reg said "One day for the funeral and wake, two days drinking and two days recovering. You don't think that Walter's imagination was stirred by the fact that one of the biggest pits around here is called Carlton quite a popular name in these parts."

"No for a 75 year old he seemed very on the ball."

Renton went back to his office and rang DS Jackson.

DS Jackson said "Frank Carlyle is now retired and there is no sign of any van much less a Commer parked anywhere near the address. He and his wife use buses and the odd taxi .Also we cannot find anything that shows that Frank and Evelyn have ever been married."

Renton hung up and returned to the collators and relayed the conversation to Frank and Reg.

Reg said "I will contact my man in the records office and hopefully have something for the afternoon debrief."

4pm arrived and all were seated mugs in hand. They were joined by Austin.

Tina said "We had a look around various places but on the way back coming out of Lincoln we stopped at a garage and the owner said that he had a white Commer van come in on Easter Sunday. He didn't clock the number but he did say that although the van was tatty he could see the word Carpentry on the side. When I asked him what did the man look like, I showed him the photographs but he was very vague and didn't pick out anyone we gave him our telephone number and said to ring if he saw the van again."

Renton said "Righto that's good so we can have that description circulated through the Ridings, stop and search."He then said "Reg what about your pal in the records office?"

"I wouldn't say pal exactly. Evelyn married William Carlyle in 1933. Derek was born 3rd May 1934.
William enlisted in 1939 in the army and once the Paras were formed in 1940 he joined them straightaway. He was one of 20 guinea pigs from March 1940 put through their paces. So I then contacted someone else and he was in the same unit as Alistair Duggan senior. This was top secret training which took place in Scotland. Originally paras jump off a static line, but as they became more experienced it was decided to try the ripcord the idea being that the para could land where he wanted to. Also they could descend more rapidly then pull the ripcord nearer the ground. My informant says this was a bit off the wall at the time. But using the static line one particular day they jumped but Carlyle's chute didn't open and he hit the deck and died..

"Ok Reg so what's the punch line." said Austin.

"During training they trained in pairs and each man would pack his own chute and then check his partners. Later the chutes were packed by woman. Guess who was Carlyle's partner yes Alistair Duggan senior."

"Revenge." said Jack.

"I wouldn't jump the gun just yet, so was there an official enquiry?" said Renton

Reg said "What do you think not a chance, fortunes of war and all that."

"Right then Steve me and you to see Duggan senior tomorrow, I will give him a call. Also I think it is time the Mets had a cosy chat with Evelyn and Frank."

Renton returned to the collators and said to Steve. I will pick you up tomorrow and see Farmer Duggan and then on Friday we will pay a surprise visit to Inkerman ourselves."

37
Ripcord

Renton picked up Steve from home and once again made their way to the Duggan farm. They stopped in Bawtry where Renton paid for a couple of bacon rolls and a Victorian sponge cake. They arrived at the farm and having parked off the road were led into the farmhouse by Alex. Once inside Helen made a flask of coffee and sliced the cake.

Once settled Renton said "What I am about to ask you I would like complete honesty from you Mr Duggan because I want you to tell me about your training in the Parachute Regiment and William Carlyle."

There was a stunned silence and glances were exchanged between Alex and his dad.

Duggan said "When we started training it was an experiment. Churchill had studied the idea of the German Stormtrooper's and decided that is what England needed in the war with Germany. Initially there was 20 of us training and we would eventually be the trainers of all those to come which by 1942 the Parachute Regiment would be ready. We trained to jump from a static line and then the time had come to do freefall and pull the ripcord. The idea being to get to land as quickly as possible and silently. We were paired up and taught to pack our own chutes together and to check each others pack. Bill and I were from two different regiments and got on really well. We made a pact to stick together through the war and come out alive together. So it came to the jump using the ripcord but something went wrong, his chute didn't open and he died."

"Was there any sort of an enquiry?" said Renton.

"No, it was all very secret mainly because if we weren't up to it then it would remain a secret. The training was very intense, I mean we did all the commando stuff before we even got near a parachute."

"Did Bill have any doubts about the training or the way the war was developing?"

"He was quite well read and had been following the course the Nazi's were taking from 1933. We were very close and he confided in me that he thought his brother was having an affair with his wife Evelyn. He said his brother was the golden boy in the family and could do no wrong and would probably carry on the business if he died. The family had decided Francis would run the business and he Bill would enlist."

"Was he worried about dying and leaving his son Derek?"

"We were all worried about dying but you joined up to fight for your country. He said if anything happened to him he knew Evelyn would bring up his son."

Renton said "Do you think Derek Carlyle resents the fact his dad died and you didn't."

Duggan nodded to Alex who went upstairs and then returned with a letter he gave to his dad.

"This arrived in 1960 you can see the postmark." He handed it to Renton.

He opened the letter and read "Now you know the pain of losing someone you love and idolise. I was five years old. Do you even remember Bill Carlyle?"

"Very short, no address and not signed, what do you think about that?"

Duggan said "I think he thinks I killed his dad so he killed my son. I didn't kill his dad, Bill and I were very close."

"We now have forensic evidence that Campbell killed Stewart or was an accessory to murder and that either killed or was an accessory to the killing of Cooper and Horton because of the way they were killed but either he or Carlyle killed Crowley alias Kowalski. Tomorrow me and my DI are going to London to see Frank and Evelyn Carlyle. I am hoping that his mum knows where he is. Thank you for your time once again I will keep you up to what is happening." said Renton.

They then returned to the station Frank said "The Commer van has been circulated in the Three Ridings and I contacted DS Jackson and he has had it circulated in the Met area."

"Righto then we are off to Inkerman tomorrow and the rest of you just circulate out in a radius of 30 miles usual thing petrol stations cafes and pubs see if anyone has seen Campbell and Carlyle."

38
London

With Ted driving, Renton and Frank went to London. They stopped near Croydon Airport for a cup of tea coffee for Renton and a sandwich. Having arrived at the Carlyle's Ted dropped them off and then went to Norwood Police Station to see DS Jackson.

Renton introduced himself and Frank to Mr. Carlyle and showed his ID card. They were shown into the lounge and Mrs Carlyle went into the kitchen. They sat down and Renton looked around. Although not luxurious it gave off a warm feel of a family home. On the sideboards was a selection of family photographs but only one of Derek Carlyle in school uniform. Mrs Carlyle came in with a trolley with cups and pieces of cake and biscuits.

"Good heavens you must be famished after that long drive from Yorkshire." She poured out the drinks and gave them a slice of cake each.

Renton said "Do you mind if my colleague makes some notes?"

Mr Carlyle said "No not at all, I suppose you being here is about Derek we have had policemen here before about him."

"Yes it is." said Renton "Can you just tell us about Derek from birth to now?"

Mr Carlyle said "Derek was 6 years old when his father William died in a training accident with the Parachute Regiment. The inquest decided that it was an accidental death something like that."

"And you married Evelyn after his death?"

"William was my brother Dad had a very successful carpentry business most of the shop fronts in Crystal Palace were built by his company. Bill and I were twins so we both went into the business from about 14 years. The business was very good before the war and busier after. But in 1939 Bill enlisted in the army. He was a determined person and Derek is the same. So it was down to dad and me to run the business. I was excused military service because I have asthma and I am colour blind. After Bill died I proposed to Evelyn and we were married and we had Derek to think about."

"Did Derek join in with the carpentry work?"

"Oh yes but unbeknown to us Derek really resented me stepping into his dad's shoes so to speak.

When the police had come to say about the inquest results Derek said I was glad his dad had died so I could get the business The resentment continued but he hid it away. He took to the carpentry very well but when he was 17 he was in a pub and got into a fight and he severely injured the other person and ended up in Borstal. After that episode we had policeman knocking on our door a few times. When he was called up for National Service we thought that might straighten him out a bit. Once he had gone, Evelyn sorted out his bedroom and found a box in the wardrobe it had an account in a newspaper about the tragic death of Bill and an account from his best mate Alistair Duggan."

"So did he hold Alistair Duggan responsible for his dad's death?"

"Oh yes, he had drawings in the box and one showed Mr Duggan with a knife in his head and covered in blood it was quite graphic."

"So did he return from Germany when his Service had finished.?"

"No we think he stayed in Germany. We didn't see or hear from him for years, until last year when he came back with a friend drunk just for the night. Evelyn cooked them breakfast in the morning then he demanded the keys of the Commer van. He went upstairs and got the box out of the wardrobe, his room was just like when he had left. He took some clothes and then wanted some of his dad's tools which he took out of the garage. He then said "I know you have sold the business so I want my share of dad's money, I think £2000 should do it for now."

"Did you give him the money?"

"£1500."

"What did his friend look like?"

"6 feet tall, well built like a rugby player, he had a slight accent maybe Scots or Irish had a beard."

Renton showed them the group photograph and Frank pointed out Carlyle and Campbell.

"Could you give me the index number of the van?"

"I can do better than that." He produced a photograph of the van.

"Was Derek homosexual?"

"I think he liked both sexes." Said Frank

Renton said "I will keep you informed about what is happening with Derek."

Evelyn said "Don't bother a leopard never changes his spots. The last time we saw him was just the same as when he went for his National Service. One thing after Bill died Mr Duggan rang us and told us what had actually happened. He rang us again in 1956 to tell us about his son dying and he thought Derek and his cronies were involved in that. We weren't surprised were we Frank?"

He nodded.

"Righto well thank you for what you have told us, if he does contact you here is my telephone number, please call me."

When they arrived back at the station Renton went in to the collators knowing Reg would still be there. "So what is your excuse for still being here then Reg?"

"Bridge night, the good lady has several of her friends round and they play a few "rubbers" whatever that is. The most I ever got to was cribbage and bridge is so much more of a bind. Then the real point of the evening will be a glass of wine and dig the dirt for their friends who didn't turn up. From that look on your face you have a request I think."

"Yes, here is the index number of the Commer van can you check it out and then pass it around the three Ridings and also contact DS Jackson to give it out to the Met. Also can you do a ring round briefing tomorrow at 11am and now my tongue is saying I should go and caress it with a pint of Yorkshire bitter before last orders."

39
Not the Pigman

At 11.15am Renton arrived in their briefing room to find everyone seated with a drink in their hand. Reg handed him a mug of steaming black coffee. He took a sip and said "On Thursday as you know Steve and I went yet again to see the Duggan's. So Steve over to you and tell us about our conversation."

Steve then related the conversation about the parachute death of Carlyle senior. When he had finished Frank said "So this letter he sent to the Duggan's is virtually a confession of what he did to Duggan junior in Germany."

Renton said "Well yes we could view it as that but would a judge and jury think it was enough to add to what we have for a guilty decision. But remember it isn't signed there is no address or who it is from. So it could have come from anyone. So moving on yesterday we went to Inkerman and spoke to Mr and Mrs Carlyle. They furnished us with a photograph of the Commer van and the number has been circulated in Yorkshire and the Met by Reg"

Reg said "May I interject?" Renton nodded. Reg continued "It would appear that Frank Carlyle had the number shown as being scrapped so maybe a bit of revenge on Derek."

Renton said "It would seem that from an early age Derek resented Uncle Frank moving into his dad's bed and marrying his mum. Between that and National Service he ended up in Borstal for beating the shit out of another and before that absenting himself from school. Mum and Uncle Frank were hoping National Service would straighten him out a bit but once finished he didn't return home. The next time they see him was about a year ago and he turns up drunk with a mate and from the description it has to be Campbell. This was confirmed by Frank pointing them out on the group photo. Next day Carlyle demands the keys to the van and £2000 and some of his dad's tools. He knew that they had sold the business, how I do not know. So there we are."

Frank said "We could suppose that Carlyle and his cronies separately are blackmailing Crowley .In the meantime Campbell bumps of the three wise monkeys and Carlyle bumps off Crowley with or without Campbell."

Renton said "That would be just too neat for my liking. We need to get that van and hopefully someone driving it. The Chief has said that if we do get just the van he will release it as a further step in the investigation just to keep the squawkers at bay. From the Home Secretary all the way down to Doubting Thomas who has now gone hurrah."

Jack said "The last time we had a sighting of a murderer was by pig man. He will be in the Diner at 1 o clock I will give him the Commer's number."

"Oh no not the pig man again" said Renton "Let's knock off for some lunch and then call it a day for you lot at 5pm, don't forget paperwork on your travels over the last few days."

Renton went out for lunch and went for a stroll in Sandall Beat Wood, lots of people walking, kids playing football. He looked at his watch 3 o clock so he went back to the station knowing Reg would be in his office. Sure enough he was there going through the card system they were using for the murders.

"Ha ha Ralph you wouldn't believe it but there has been a sighting of a very dirty Commer van with that index number in Bradford."

"Does the pig man's range extend that far then." said Renton laughing.

"Bill Barclay the collator put that number out to all and sundry. However a bobby who had been doing rugby training for the juniors was back on duty at 11 am. He was on a road bridge looking down at the traffic and saw this dirty Commer van and thought you don't often see a white one so clocked the number for future reference. He went back in the nick for refs and mentioned it to Bill who rang me.

They have asked for a photograph of the van. Peter is running a couple off as we speak."

"Righto. I think Jack and Dennis are on duty tomorrow so can you get a hold of them and they can pick up the copies and take them to Bradford David and Tina to Leeds and Ted and Peter Johns to Wakefield."

The telephone rang Reg answered it and then scribbled something on his note pad.

"That garage that Tina went to coming out of Lincoln the owner was talking to his son who is the mechanic there. Apparently the son got a clear view of the driver as he left so dad has asked if Tina could go back and show the son the photographs."

"Excellent David and Tina can do that one on their way back from Leeds."

40
A Wager

Renton arrived at his desk at 9am knowing that he would have some files to sort out and mark up for court. It being a Sunday he hoped he wouldn't be disturbed. The Chief was day off so morning prayers would be just Chief Inspector Fox, the DI and a DS. Two files later it was time for a coffee so he went down to the collators to find it empty. He could see the notepad that contained the scrawls and doodles that Reg put in from the previous day but no Reg. He made himself a coffee and 10 minutes later Reg walked in.

"Toilet." said Renton

"No rushed out of the house and forgot my sandwiches."

"Escaping?"

"Yes, Mrs P has her beloved twin sister coming over with her son, an obnoxious creature. He has this attitude that he knows everything and something that you don't he is studying to be a social worker, God help the public when he qualifies."

Just then Oskar walked in.

Renton said "Short wake?"

"Yes you can only take so much what a great chap he was and what a pity that the regiment has lost such a good man. So how are we getting on with the murders done and dusted?"

After he had a drink Renton and Reg brought him up to speed.

"Great so have we got a bet on who will be nicked driving the Commer?" said Oskar.

Renton said "I think we will give that a miss Sergeant Peplinski. I shall return to my paperwork." With that he went back to his office.

Oskar said "Shouldn't we be swamping Bradford and getting out there?

Reg said "Big area Bradford and includes the moors lot of open country. The van was sighted going out of Bradford at least the road that goes out could be anywhere."

Oskar said "I bet you a fiver that the van is being used by Carlyle?"

Reg said "Done." They shook hands."Now sod off and let me get on with this paperwork."

It was the 4pm debrief and everyone was in waiting for Renton to appear.

Once he was seated he said "So what have you lot got for me?"

There was silence except for Tina who said "We went to the garage and saw the owner's son he picked out Campbell as the driver. I asked him if there was an identification parade would he be able to pick him out. He said no problem."

"Righto let's call it a day and see you all tomorrow."

41
You owe me a fiver

It was Monday the 4th July 1966 the days had passed into weeks and months. The Chief had scaled back the investigation with just Renton, Steve and Reg assigned to any information coming in. Frank Oskar and Tina were back on CID, Jack and Dennis back on uniform duties.

Austin came in for a brew and said to Reg "Just you today Reg?"

"Steve is out following up an enquiry, Ralph and Jenny are in York today for an official funeral some high ranking brass who has been retired for donkeys. He will be back tomorrow,"

Just then the collator's telephone rang, Reg answered it in his official tone then said "Bloody hell Smudge, yes Ralph is away but I will call him. I will get onto Doc Wells and Peter. I will get Frank and Oskar to you soon as." He hung up and then said to Austin "Body in a white Commer van in a garage in South Elmsall somewhere near the railway station."

Austin said "That will be Bill Stinton's garage."

Reg rang Doc Wells and then Peter upstairs in the fingerprint room and then Frank "Body in a white Commer van near the railway station in Elmsall. Smudge is there Pc Foxy Fowler will wave you in from Donny Road. The Doc and Peter are on their way. I am now ringing the hotel where Ralph is staying. He was going to stay an extra night, but I am sure he will be back."

5 minutes later Frank and Oskar were driving out of the police station, they could see Peter in his van ahead. Frank said "I hope this is the breakthrough we need."

Oskar said "I reckon the body is Carlyle I think he would be no match for Campbell who was built like a bull."

They drove through sleepy Hooton Pagnell and down Elmsall Lane under the old railway bridge, past the fireworks factory as they approached Foxy Fowler he waved them into the road that led to the railway station, they could see Sergeant Smith standing outside a garage with double doors. They stopped so as to block the road and as they got out of the car they saw Peter get out of his van and approached Smudge who said "Ay up lad tha must a broke the speed limit gettin' here. Let's wait for the Doc, the bugger in the van is definitely dead."

5 minutes later Doctor Wells arrived and went in the garage. Several minutes later he came out "Dead as a dodo." He signalled Peter to go, Frank and Oskar stood in the doorway. They could see the Commer was parked over an inspection pit. Doc Wells went back inside.

Oskar said to Smudge "Is this a regular garage or just a lock-up?"

"Aye it was Stinton's garage up to last year. But Bill Stinton decided it was time to give up crawling under cars and climbing in and out of that pit so he has been hiring it out as a storage place."

"Did he find the body?"

"Aye gave him a bit of a shock, all that blood he was walking their dog down t' lane and notice the window open so he unlocked this small door and then noticed the smell. So he unlocked the garage doors saw the blood and rang 999 and they sent me and Foxy. It's shook him right up so it has. I will go and get a statement when he has had a bit of a lie down. I think it brought on a bit of shell shock from D Day. His lass Agnes is not a woman to be messed wi so she has sent him to bed."

Peter shouted out "Its Carlyle."

Oskar said to Frank and Smudge "So just Campbell to get a hold of then, did he rent the garage?"

Smudge said "I showed Bill the photo of Campbell but he said the feller that rented the garage had a black beard and dark hair to match. He rented it in April and said he would need it to August gave Bill the four months up front."

Just then Doc Wells came out. "I would say he had been dead for up to 6 weeks maybe a bit less the post mortem will confirm that. I would say he was strangled with the wire his head is almost severed then placed in the box in the corner with some familiar rope and covered with some sacking. Then transferred to the van, possibly to eventually move it and dump it. The mortuary team should be here soon I said to give me a 30 minute head start. Got to go cheery bye you chaps."

Oskar said "Does he talk like that all the time.?"

"Aye but a bloody good doctor for all that." said Smudge.

Frank and Oskar went in the garage and Peter said "Strangled but not with a wire."

Frank said "He was the last one of the pack so no need to leave it on display. Did Bill give you any sort of description of who hired the garage?"

Smudge "said "What before he fainted, Foxy had to catch the dog, ha ha. He said abaht 6 foot well built had a rugby shirt on, this was in June, said his accent weren't Yorkshire or Southern posh but faintly Irish or maybe Scots, but a quiet voice, not someone he would mess wi."

Frank said "Peter will carry on here and if Foxy could keep the nosey parkers away and lock up when Peter has finished. I will sort something out to get the Commer picked up tomorrow."

"Aye no sweat, I will get that statement from Bill and drop it in."

On the way back Frank said to Oskar "I bet the hiring of the garage was all word of mouth and just a handshake no paperwork as usual.

We will have to rely on Stinton's statement but I am sure Smudger will wring the truth out of him."

In the collators later Reg said "Ralph is coming back today and will be here he hopes by 4pm for a briefing, so I have contacted Tina, Jack and Dennis so they can do house to house with Smudger's lads. He said can you go and brief the Chief."

Oskar said "You owe me a fiver?"

"Why?" said Reg.

"Because the van was found with Carlyle in it."

Reg winked at Frank and said "Perhaps it a bit technical for an ex-squaddie but the alive last occupant was Campbell so you owe me a fiver young man. So put the kettle on for a nice pot of tea for when Frank gets back from the Chief."

Day 82 Frank returned from seeing the Chief and relating that the body in the van was Derek Carlyle. Reg handed him a strong tea in his Coldstream Guards mug. He took a swig and said "Guess what I have finally got Steve to go to a post mortem, I did suggest the vaseline up the nose trick. The Chief has sanctioned that we get the old team back together so they should all be here for the 4pm debrief."

Reg said "Ralph has cut short the funeral and arranged for someone else to do the honours and to make up for the extra night in York he is taking Jenny to lunch and then back here soon to be married so getting in practice how to placate the wife ha ha."

Just then in walked Sergeant Smudge Smith, seeing Reg having some sandwiches he said "Hoho am I just in time for some snap?" (Snap was a miners term they put their food in a snap tin which had a clip to keep the lid in place so the rats couldn't get at the food.)

Reg offered him an apple.

"Nay lad's just a lid of tea and one for the lad ere."
(Lid was a miners term for the lid on the snap tin)

Frank said "So for what do we owe this honour Smudge."

"I have the statement from Bill Stinton who is recovering from finding a smelly body in his lock-up. That lad of yours Peter, my God he is thorough. Arnold here" he pointed to the constable "drove the Commer back, but we couldn't find a key and Peter wouldn't let me look through the corpse's clothes until he had finished taking photographs and measurements .He is going to do a scaled drawing of the body's position in the van as well as the photos."

"So how do you start and drive a vehicle without a key?"said Oskar

"Ee lad thas got a lot to learn its all done be me magic key which fits any car, van or lorry." He touched his nose and winked at Frank."I showed Bill the group photo and imagine yon feller wi dark hair and a dark beard could that be the feller who hired the garage. He said it could be the man. He can't even remember the name the feller gave."

Frank said "So when we come down tomorrow and do the usual house to house will we be in luck."

"That road leads to the station and for cars is a dead end. There is parking for folk using the trains and for walking their dogs or taking kids int park. There is the old mill building which is disused and further down the lane are two houses, the Stationmasters Wally Johnson and t'other is Stan Clements the signalman. The lane goes into fields and then out onto Donny Road further down almost to fireworks factory."

Frank said "So we haven't got a lot on the person who hired the garage Smudger?"

"Bill said that this feller had a tattoo on his arm quite distinct, he thought it were the word Honour And F or summat like that. He couldn't see the third word."

"That's interesting." said Oskar "Honour and Fidelity is the motto of the Foreign Legion."

Frank said "Do you reckon Bill would recognise him if he saw him in a line up in an identification parade?"

"Oh aye I reckon he would."

"Right well I am going to the diner for lunch, see you later Smudge."

At 3.45pm Frank walked in and saw all the team sitting enjoying a drink he was just about to speak when Renton walked in.

Renton said "So what has been happening in my absence?"

Frank then relayed to them all what had happened from the initial telephone call up to the present time. "Also Steve attended his first post mortem." there was a round of applause.

Renton said "What did you gain from that Steve apart from the smell."

Steve said "The Doc is of the opinion that there is one killer for Crowley and another for the others. He is still there and said he would furnish the report as soon as possible. For my benefit he relayed exactly what he was doing as he did it and with great relish he really enjoys his job. The box in the garage contained rope which he thinks was used on Stewart."

Just then Peter walked in and sat down.

"Renton said "What do you have for us?"

"Yes sir, the rope in the box is identical to that used on Stewart and Horton. The tire tread of the Commer's offside tyre in the garage is exactly the same as that at the shack in Sandall Beat Wood. Doctor Wells is going to compare the blood of all the victims against that of Carlyle just in case he was involved with Campbell in their killings. I found a wire in the glove compartment of the van which has a loop at either end I showed it to Doctor Wells and he is going to see if the blood on it matches any of the victims but thinks it will probably show only Horton's because he was the last to be garrotted. The Commer is now in the backyard and with daylight tomorrow I will be going over it to find any blood splashed from the killings."

Renton said "Has the doctor got an idea of when Carlyle was killed?"

"Originally he said about 6 weeks ago now that the body has been unwrapped he thinks 6 weeks or thereabouts definitely at the end of May. I managed to get Carlyle's fingerprints. Do you remember that one of the glasses in Crowley's house near the vodka bottle had slightly smeared fingerprints on it well I think it could be

Campbell's prints because they don't match Carlyle or Crowley or any of the victim's."

"Excellent Peter thank you. For the rest of us we will be going to the railway station and stopping people who are using the trains on a regular basis to go to work also any dog walkers wandering along that way. Tomorrow Tina and Jack go and see the stationmaster and see if he has seen any activity from the garage. Steve you go and see the signalman same thing. Oskar and I will be with Smudge's chaps doing the stop and ask. Austin do you know Bill Stinson?"

"Oh yes."

"Righto then at some stage I would like you to go with Peter and take the identikit case and see if he can build up a picture of Campbell. Lets not forget we are now onto day 82, nearly 3 months. If we get a good likeness for Campbell then with the permission of the brass we will have it circulated to all police stations and then published in the National Newspapers. Frank can you ring Smudge and get him to line up a couple of his lads for tomorrow. I will be in the Red Lion at 6 o clock usual drill."

As everyone got up to leave the telephone rang Reg answered it and passed it to Renton "Doctor Wells for you."

Doctor Wells said "Just thought you should know Carlyle had been tied up in a chair, there was one in the garage and systematically worked over. Broken nose same for the cheekbones, broken jaw several teeth knocked out. Then strangled the killer probably told him why he was going to kill him."

43
South Elmsall

It was 9am and everyone was at South Elmsall railway station .After a short pep talk from Renton Austin and Peter accompanied by Smudge Smith went to see Bill Stinson to try and build up a picture of Campbell. Tina and Jack went to see the station master, Steve went to the signal box. Two Constables from South Kirkby arrived and were then positioned to ask people at the rail station if they had seen any vehicles or people hanging around outside the garage. Renton went for a stroll along Doncaster Road and went into St Mary's Church to find the vicars wife who made him a cup of coffee and forced a scone on him. He then went back out and Peter arrived to say they had managed to get an identikit of Campbell.

"But to be honest sir it just looks like his training photo but with darker hair and a black beard. I am going back to the office and will photograph it and then print off some photos but they won't be ready until at least 3pm."

"That's okay Peter you go back and I will see you at the collator's later." said Renton.

Smudge had prearranged for some sandwiches at the Chequers Public House and at 1pm everyone was in the back room with sandwiches, buns and mugs of tea or coffee.

Once everyone had eaten Renton said "I would like to thank our local constables for their efforts today it is a thankless task but we only need one or two people to have seen Carlyle or Campbell at the garage neither the station master or the signalman have been of any use. So what I propose is that this continues every day this week. Start at 8am to 12 midday to catch those going to work early and then from 4pm to 6pm. David and Tina to do those shifts in case a statement is needed. I will be back at Doncaster and if you get a breakthrough I am sure Smudge will give me a call.
Also tomorrow we hope to have some photographs of Carlyle and Campbell for you to show the public."

When they had finished their lunch the two constables went out. Renton said "I had a telephone call yesterday from the God called Bullstone who is of the opinion that Campbell is still in this country. How he knows God knows. Tomorrow when we have the prints of Campbell from the identikit, if Jack could deliver some to Smudge and his boys and the rest of you will be in Doncaster with them. The Chief will then be deciding if and when the print is given to the National Newspapers."

Renton was just about to get in the car to return to the station when in the distance looking at the garage doors was none other than Alfie Wormald. Renton walked down towards him and said "Alfie can I help you?"

"Hello Mister Renton I was just wondering if there is a story here for me?"

Renton said "I spoke to the editor of the Post a while back but if you keep out of our hair I will give you the scoop of the year. What do you say?"

"Fab." said Alfie.

Renton said "Come to the police station in say one hour and ask for me in the front office, okay see you then and bring your camera."

Renton returned to the station and briefly explained to the Chief about his idea with Alfie.

"Excellent Ralph us using the press for a change."

Forty minutes later Renton and Alfie were in the backyard of the police station.

Renton said "So Alfie I want you to take a photograph of this Commer van but side on and even better if you get the index number in as well. You see on the side it has very faintly the word "CAR" and then Carpentry. This van was driven by the man who we suspect is the killer. So a photograph of the van with these two photographs."

He gave Alfie the small photograph copies of Carlyle and Campbell and said "In the explanation I want you to type something like "Have you seen this vehicle with either of these two men. If so please contact Doncaster Police" That's all nothing else. I will ring your editor and you can do the rest. If you do this we will give you the basic story about these murders after the killer is convicted what do you say?"

Alfie said "Wow thank you Mister Renton this will set me up as a real reporter. He vigorously shook Renton's hand.

Renton then watched him take the photograph of the van and then led him back onto the street. He then went inside and rang the editor of the Post and went down to the collators. Having made a drink he asked Reg what was the latest.

Reg said "A while ago I gave all the details of our victims and Carlyle and Campbell to our contact in the Foreign Office. He speaks several languages, ex copper injured in the line of duty and someone with half an ounce of common sense put him in this office with several different telephones. So he went through his files from 1956 to 1965 and then up to now. Not counting Crowley, Cooper Stewart and Horton never left our shores apart from National Service. Crowley used a variety of names but always the same date of birth, travelled to Paris and Amsterdam so perhaps that had something to do with the diamonds."

"Okay get to the point."

"Ha ha both Carlyle and Campbell had trips back to England and then went to Paris and Algiers. Didn't we have information that Campbell had a tattoo relating to the Foreign Legion which has an office in Paris and Algiers."

"Yes Honour and Fidelity."

"My contact says that Campbell doesn't appear to have come back to England but a Francois Durand with the same date of birth as Campbell has come back to England recently."

"Great stuff enough secret service for now let's talk tomorrow. I had better go and see the Chief and see what he is up to with the press boys."

44
Francois Durand

Renton arrived at his office, looked through his in tray and changed the calendar Monday 11th July 1966. Almost a week had passed and nothing further had come to light on the whereabouts of James Campbell. He looked at the pile of files in the in tray awaiting his attention, but first a good strong hot black coffee was needed so down to the collators where he made a coffee.

Reg said "The Chief still dithering over whether to put Campbell's mug in the papers, then?"

"Yes I hope this murder enquiry is not going the same way as others we have had............."

Before he could finish his sentence the collator's telephone rang. Reg answered it listened and said "Yes sir of course sir I will find him and pass on your message, yes sir excellent news."

He put the receiver down "The Chief wetting his knickers can you go and see him Campbell has been arrested in Brighton."

Renton said "Get everyone together here in 30 minutes." He then went upstairs.

"Aha Ralph please sit down, well great news. Campbell has been arrested in Brighton on the south coast, so that means we don't have to use the press and thank God for that. Their Chief rang me and said for you to telephone a Superintendent Carter who will explain all. So over to you here is his number."

Renton went to his office and telephone the officer after the usual polite chat. Superintendent Carter then explained how Campbell had been arrested.

30 minutes later was back in the collators to find everyone there drinks in hand.

"Righto well good news Campbell is in custody in Brighton Police Station which is in their Town Hall. He was arrested on Saturday lunchtime in a pub having got into a fight. Police attended and he assaulted a Police Sergeant and it took four of them to get him into a van. He was taken to the hospital and had his face stitched up possibly summary justice. Got him back to the cop shop where he calmed down and actually gave his fingerprints. So they thought they were dealing with a French hooligan because he said his name was Francois Durand. But the two passports the CID found at his girlfriend's address showed the same mug shot for a Francois Durand and a James Campbell. Also at the address was almost a thousand pounds in cash and in his briefcase a small pouch of 5 uncut diamonds. His female companion was also arrested but released and she showed the CID where the money and the diamonds were. Nothing like a woman scorned. I think when she found out that her lover was not French and was a murderer she decided it was time for a bit of revenge."

"Very public spirited of her." said Austin.

"Yes I thought so. A DS remembered something about a James Campbell so they rushed his fingerprints to the Yard and Ted's mate confirmed that this is the James Campbell wanted by us. So Campbell is in court today where he will be found guilty and fined £250 with some costs taken out of his thousand pounds. So their Chief has said we can have him tomorrow but send a few and I quote "Burly chaps." They will only sign him over to an Inspector so tomorrow Frank, Jack and Ted to drive down to Brighton and bring him back here. Don't question him but if he does say anything after he has been cautioned then write it down. He will be housed in the cell we used for Michel Morton and then go into the larger cell next to it to be interviewed. Frank and I will do the first interviews and Steve making the notes. If he buggers around speaking French I will interview him in French. For the later interviews it will be me and Oskar and see if he recognises you we will start the interviews tomorrow. The fact that he has obviously been living it up since the last murder I think shows he doesn't give a damn but Jack Ted and Dennis to do the suicide watch."

Frank, Jack and Ted arrived back at the police station at 6.30pm with Campbell handcuffed to Jack. He was shown down to the cellblock where Renton and Dennis were waiting for him. One the two gates were locked he was released from the handcuff's, he was shown into his cell. His property was taken and put in the property cupboard and locked. Frank and Jack went back upstairs

Renton said "I am Superintendent Renton and you are now my responsibility and I will be one of the interviewing officers. We have saved you a meal from our canteen." Renton then repeated it in French.

Campbell said in English "I am bloody starving, so yes please."

Dennis brought in the meal and they watched him wolf it down, Dennis gave him a mug of tea.

Campbell took a drink and said "So what happens now?"

Renton said "Tomorrow we will start interviewing you about the murders that have happened here in Doncaster. If we decide you are the murderer you will be charged and then be taken to court and remanded until you appear in the assizes but there is a good chance it could be the Old Bailey in London. If found guilty you will go to prison the length of your sentence will be determined by the judge so we will see you tomorrow at 10 am. There is a jailer on 24 hours a day if you need anything. Is there anyone you would like me to contact."

"No they are all dead."

"Would you like me to inform a solicitor so you can have legal advice?"

"Solicitors bloody vultures feeding off the underdogs, no thanks. Do you have any reading material?"

45
First Interview

Renton, Frank and Steve went into the interview room and sat down, Colin Turton who had just started his shift brought in Campbell.

Renton said "I must remind you that you are still under caution ." He then read it out and then said "Do you wish a solicitor to be present for this interview?"

"No." said Campbell.

Renton said "Can I call you James?"

"Yeah fine."

"Righto, I am Detective Superintendent Renton, this is Detective Inspector Dipper and this is Detective Sergeant Bowers who will be taking notes which will be typed out for you to read and then sign. The time is 10.05am on Thursday 14th July 1966."As he spoke he noticed the tattoo "Honour and Fidelity."

"When you were arrested in Brighton all your clothing had been taken from you were given this clothing. All your original clothing is being examined by Doctor Wells and will also be photographed."

Campbell shrugged his shoulders.

Renton said "I won't patsy around we know you killed Cooper, Stewart, Horton and Carlyle and possibly Kowalski. We have evidence but I want to hear from you why and how you murdered them."

"I didn't kill Kowalski that was Carlyle's doing. I hated Kowalski for being the ringleader who probably gave the order to kill my cousin although I think he was ordered to do it from the Russians or maybe the Stasi. But Carlyle really hated him all he said all the time was how he was going to kill him."

Frank said "When did you find out that Alistair was your cousin."

"Although my father contacted me after Al died, Al told me that we were cousins about 4 weeks or so before he died."

"Did he confide in you about what he had found out about Carlyle and his chums?" said Renton

"He found out that Cooper who was working in the orderly room come post bunk and was sifting through military dispatches and various communiques, he was then passing it on to Stewart who was the errand boy who then passed it on to Carlyle who then passed it to his oppo Kowalski. Stewart passed it to Carlyle outside the barracks in various cafes. He was then passing it to a Stasi agent in the nightclub in Berlin. Stewart thought I was a German working for the Stasi and told me one drunken night the system they were using."

"We have talked to Alistair's dad but what did you think of Alistair?"

"He was a lovely lad he was doing a science degree but wanted to be a doctor. I told him to keep his head down and keep away from Carlyle and the other creeps, do his service and then go to university. But after he lost his stripe he went a bit mental in trying to prove that Carlyle and his gang were traitors. He could be very principled or is that stubborn?"

"What happened that made him lose his stripe?"

Carlyle was a devious bastard and very switched on and I think he twigged that Al knew about them. So he gets all friendly, he could be charming when he needed to be and then they take Al to the Blue Iguana, get him drunk slip him a couple of sleepers. He is out cold and they put him to bed and lock him in. They had a couple of rooms in the basement. He is in there for at least 24 hours in which time he is posted absent without leave. They release him and he goes back to barracks. Gets arrested then up in front of the adjutant on Company Orders, confined to barracks and demoted. When I had a word with Stewart he spilled the beans the little shit. I think it was a bit over the top he had only been absent overnight but Kowalski had a few people in his pocket"

Renton said "When you say you had a word with Stewart do you actually mean you tortured him?"

"You say tortured I say had a word. He told me about Kowalski telling Carlyle how to fix the rifle so it blew back into Al's face. Carlyle set it up with Horton's rifle everyone knew from training that Horton was shit at cleaning and sorting his kit. How many times did Al help Horton with his kit and he does this to him."

Frank said "So at the time Alistair died did you have an inkling about what really happened.?"

"No, I was undercover by this time and my contact met me and told me what had happened that Al had died due to a misfire. I knew a couple of squaddies who were linked to the orderly office and they told me that Cooper had intimated that it wasn't all that kosher. My contact told me later what had happened and I put two and two together. At the time Stewart told me about the set up I wanted to kill the little rat there and then."

"So what were you actually doing undercover in Berlin?"

"About 2 months before I started training at Catterick information had come through about what was going on at Berlin. There had been information that various people of a Russian persuasion were trying to get information out of soldiers about what their dispositions were, movements within Germany, remember the Cold War was in full swing. I was getting bored at University and wanted some action so I had applied to join MI6 my dad had a friend who was in the service and got me the interview I and then they approached me with the idea of doing the MI6 training and then training at Catterick then going undercover. My cover would be that I had deserted and being a German speaker I could use that to my advantage. The initial information was that German Nationals backed by the Stasi were setting up the various high ranking officers but they then found out it was being run by someone from inside the barracks it transpired it was Kowalski who was running it. He quickly identified Carlyle as being useful and Cooper being in the orderly office was gold dust to them. Stewart as I said was their runner and they didn't trust bonehead Horton they just used him as muscle at the club. Anyway I got quite familiar with a waitress in the Iguana and she overheard a conversation between Kowalski and Carlyle talking to a couple of villains and said that he and Carlyle were celebrating having got rid of a nagging cancer in the barracks, it had to be about Al."

Renton said "So you finished National Service and what did you do then, the French connection I mean?" he pointed to the tattoo on Campbell's arm.

"My father wanted me to go and work for him in South Africa. But we never really got on I stuck it for a couple of months. In the local bar you used to get mercenaries coming in for a beer and I got talking to one of them. He was ex Foreign Legion and suggested I join up and see the world. So I did. I was lucky in being fluent in French because they teach you to speak French the hard way with a very large stick or a punch in the guts. I passed out and I was in the Regiment. After 3 months they said did I want to do a bit of instructing in a training regiment. I thought it might be in Paris. Wrong it was in the desert of course and who should I find has just joined up but Carlyle. By this time I had discovered that he and the others had all been complicit in Al's death so I thought I would bide my time and find out where the others were and at a later date exact some revenge. We became big mates whoring drinking and fighting together. I gradually found out what had been going on in Berlin, he had a very loose tongue when he was pissed. As I got to know him I realised that he hated Cooper Stewart and Horton and Kowalski almost as much as me so I thought if I feed that desire to kill he might just do the job and then ultimately when they were all dead I could finish him off myself."

"So you freely admit to killing Carlyle?"

"Oh God yes it was a pleasure to rid the world of another scumbag."

"So who was Francois Durand?"

"Ha ha yes. He was my training sergeant. His real name was Hermann Crump, he had been in the SS during the war but after Stalingrad he deserted and joined the Legion very able soldier, he showed me how to double the wire and choke the bastards. We got chopped up in an ambush Hermann got shot to pieces. When he died I borrowed his passport, it has some in very useful with my details on it. Apart from Al, Hermann was the only true friend I could trust."

"Why did Carlyle join the Legion then?"

"Things started hotting up in Berlin. Kowalski and Dekko were setting up high ranking brass and blackmailing them for info and eventually a French Colonel went to the authorities and the wheels of justice started to investigate. The Russians paid Kowalski in diamonds and dollars. He in turn paid Dekko in cash and I think they were probably bedding buddies. However Kowalski did a runner leaving Dekko to face the music. He managed to get out by the skin of his teeth he always said he had money in various places I thought he was just bragging but he must have had to get to Paris and enlist. He said that once he had done his time in the Legion he would track down Kowalski and get his money and kill him. Eventually we were discharged from the Legion and he took me to see his mum and Uncle Frank, Dekko hated him as well. Dekko had been sleeping with some army guy in Berlin who joined the police in London he found out for him where Cooper and Stewart were living so we decided we would use them to find the others. Dekko said "But I want Kowalski the most I will make that bastard pay." He went on and on about him. It was a pleasure to eventually shut him up."

"Righto we will leave it there for now."

"Is there any chance of some reading material, like the Financial Times and the Daily Telegraph, you have my money, I can pay."

"I will get today's and drop them into the jailer later."

Colin then took Campbell back to his cell.

Renton said to Colin "Keep an eye on him don't trust him an inch remember he sees killing a person like we swat a fly."

"Yes sir, he is a big bugger."

Later in the murder room Frank said "Are we going to let him continue with this story about how Carlyle killed the others?"

Renton said "Yes because he will tell us how they went about it when really it was him doing the killing but you never know. The fact that he has admitted killing Carlyle which we know in his mind he doesn't mind being charged as an accessory to the others also did you notice he said it was a pleasure to rid the world of another scumbag. Steve can you nip out and get him the Financial Times and a Daily Telegraph and a Post for me.

2nd Interview

Renton arrived at his desk at 8.30am and found several files waiting for his approval to be ticked off for court one of rape and several for breaking and entering. He decided to look through the rape file but decided that the others could be sorted out by Chief Inspector Fox. One hour later he was satisfied with what he had seen of the rape file and placed that in the tray to be picked up by the prosecutions team. He decided it was time for a strong black coffee. The post boy came in and said "Morning sir only a postcard for you from that berk in America."

Renton picked it up it was from Robert Bond in Rio. On it was written "Happy days here in the land of sun and pink gins." He tore it in half and then went down to the collators. Frank was there talking to Reg.

"Another bloody postcard from Bond."

As he made the coffee Reg said "I hope the postmark was Rio and not London, Ralph."

"Could we be so lucky that he was here in Britain. I have the Post here and Alfie has done a good job and stuck to what I said." said Renton.

Reg looked at the item with the van and the two photographs and said "Excellent let's hope we get some quality witnesses and not the usual loonies. So how are you getting on with our mass murderer?"

Renton said "We have established that he was on the path of revenge and that he cultivated his friendship with Carlyle to track down his victims as Carlyle was looking for Howell. He admitted he tortured Stewart to find out where the others were. Stewart also told him about young Alistair being set up for his death. He is saying that he went along with Carlyle who killed them all but he freely admits to killing Carlyle."

Oskar came in and made himself a drink and said "When do I get a crack at him?"

"The problem is Oskar that when he sees you will he shut up and stop talking because he knows that you know all about him, let's see how we get on today. Here are two breaking and entering files could you go over them and see if they are ready for court if they are I will sign them up but they must be perfect. Once we have had him sign the statements then you can come in and see if he recognises you. Ready Frank shall we go and see our murderer."

Oskar said "It has really been bugging me where Kowalski got the name Harold Crowley. I finally realised Harold Crowley was one of the sergeant majors at the barracks."

They went down to the cellblock. Renton said to Colin the jailor "Anything untoward Colin?"

"No sir he has been fine he wanted a pen to do the crossword so I gave him the stub of a pencil I had and I will get that from him when he comes out."

Campbell went into the interview room and sat down. Renton said "Newspapers all good James?"

"Yes nice to catch up on my shares and see what is happening in the world outside Doncaster Police Station."

"Righto let me remind you that you are still under caution and if you wish a solicitor to be present please say so. The time for the record is 10.05 and it is Friday 15th July 1966. I have the statement you gave us and it is all typed up, would you read it, tell me if there is anything you would like to change and then sign the bottom of the pages."

Campbell read the statement and signed it.

"Righto James let's start with the first murder but first where were you and Carlyle staying over this period of the murders being committed"

"We rented a room in Doncaster above a shop."

"Can you give me the address?"

Frank wrote down the address.

"So tell me about Cooper and his end?"

"Cooper the weasel. Carlyle introduced him and Stewart to me in a pub in Doncaster. They apparently didn't recognise me from training, but they were both pissed and Carlyle just introduced me as a mate from the Legion. Carlyle was keen to go to Brighton he had invested some money in an antiques shop with one of his male friends. We dropped Stewart off at some address then took Cooper to that village and tossed a coin to who was going to do Cooper who was fast asleep in the van. We went to that cross and waited for a bit and then after midnight we dragged him out of the van and then Carlyle did the business, boy did he bleed."

Renton said "How did Carlyle kill him?"

"He used the double wire technique on him as taught to us by Hermann."

Renton said "I think you are lying. I think you did the wire treatment on him as you told him why you were killing him and do you know how we know this because you were seen alone at the butter cross seen by a witness who would recognise you in a line up. The clothes you were wearing then are the clothes you were arrested in by Brighton Police?"

"Oh alright I killed the little worm."

Renton said "Please say who the worm is?"

"Yes bloody Eric Cooper for God's sake."

"So why did you kill him in such a public place?"

"I was hoping the press would get a hold of it and it would flush out the others."

"Right let's move onto Terry Stewart we know you killed him.

"No that was Carlyle".

"Really we have a fingerprint on the new padlock that you bought to lock Stewart in where he was tied up and gagged."

Renton then produced the padlock and the confirmation of the fingerprint saying "Here is exhibits RR/1 and RR/2 have a look."

Campbell looked at them and said "Looks like you have me bang to rights but actually Carlyle asked me to get the padlock which I bought in Doncaster."

"Renton said "On the evidence we have we will charge you with the murder of Stewart. There is not a single fingerprint to show that Carlyle was in that shed or in the Commer van whereas we have your fingerprints on the steering wheel. Earlier I said that you tortured Stewart and you said you had a word with him."

"Okay one weasel less".

"Are you saying you garrotted and killed Terence Stewart?"

"Yes I am saying I garrotted and killed the little weasel called Terence Stewart do we have to go on and on like this?"

"Righto, why don't we take a break for lunch and carry on afterwards."

Campbell went back to the cell and Renton said "Type them up now Steve and we will get him to sign after lunch. Start again at 3pm."

In the collators Renton gave the address to Oskar "This room was rented by Carlyle and Campbell can you go and check it out see what is in there take Tina with you."

Oskar and Tina arrived back with a small case which was locked. They went down to the cell block and looked through Campbell's possessions and found a small key which opened the case. Inside was an envelope Renton pulled out several rolls of money and 3 passports they had Campbell's photograph in with the names of James Duggan, Otto Meier and Francois Durand. In the leather pouch was the garrotting wire.

Renton said "Take this to Peter and fingerprint the lot we need Campbell's fingerprints on the lot. Was there anything else."

Oskar said "The room was rented from Friday 1st April 1966 to Monday 11th July 1966. There was nothing in there apart from this case and sweet wrappers and newspapers."

3pm Renton, Frank and Steve were sitting in the interview as Colin brought in Campbell. Once he had sat down Renton produced the statement from the morning and asked him to read through it. He did so and signed it and said "Might as well be hung for a sheep as well as a lamb."

Renton said "So when did Carlyle surface."

Campbell said "I rang up his number in the antique shop in Brighton and told him that Cooper was dead and that I had killed Stewart but we needed to find Horton and Kowalski. He said that he had a mate in the police in London and he would see if they could track Kowalski down of course at this stage we assumed he had changed his name. I told him that Stewart had said that Horton lived in this mining village called South Elmsall and he drank in various pubs around there but also in Doncaster. So he turns up in a bloody bright red Jag the next day. I thought what a twat. He says to me he knows where Kowalski is and changed his name to Harold Crowley."

"So how did he find out where Kowalski was living?"

"Carlyle said that the info came from his contact in the police, he had to pay for it. So we go to the address that evening in the Commer not that bright red Jag. I dropped him off and then went back to the digs and picked him up the next day. Carlyle had got Kowalski pissed and they had sex and somewhere along the line he found out that Kowalski had cash and diamonds hidden in the house. Carlyle said he was going to blackmail him and get some of the loot owed to him for Kowalski leaving him in Germany. So the next night which was sometime near to or after killing Stewart Saturday I think we went to Bentley and Carlyle introduces me to Kowalski and out comes the vodka. Kowalski was drinking schnapps straight from the bottle. Talking about old times all that shit then they go upstairs for a bit of you know what then all of a sudden there is this sort of a clunking noise. I rush upstairs and Kowalski is on the bed out for the count. Carlyle ties his hands and feet and positions him so his head is hanging over the end of the bed and has my wire round his neck."

Renton said "So you didn't do anything?"

"No this was down to Carlyle he had been banging on about killing him. He wakes up Kowalski with some water splashed on his face and then asks him where the money and the diamonds are, Kowalski tells him to fuck off in German. By this time Carlyle is sort of see-sawing the wire round his neck. Kowalski keeps on telling him to go to hell. Carlyle goes downstairs comes back up with a carving knife and slices open his throat blood everywhere a right mess. I tell him it's time to fuck off. I tell him to go in the bathroom and sponge some of the blood off his clothes with a towel. I go downstairs and start up the van. He gets in and we vamoose. What a bloody fiasco. I tell him to get in the Jag and bugger off which he did."

"So you took no part in actually killing Kowalski." Said Frank

"No it was his call he had been going on and on about sorting Kowalski. I went back to the digs and laid low for a couple of days and then took the van to the lock-up near the railway station then got the train down to Brighton and met Julie I turned on the French charm and moved in with her"

"So where does this technique of using the double wire to garrotte your victims come from?"

"Hermann said that originally it was perfected by a sect called the Thuggie in India. They were gangs of bandits who would follow travellers and get to know them then when they weren't expecting it they would strangle them using cloth ropes or cords. Herman refined this by doubling the wire. So twice round the throat tighten it up, knee in the lower back and pull. Very quick and almost cuts their head off. The other way was if your victim was taller or bigger than you then you twist the wire at the back turn round and bend over so the victim is off the ground and his weight does the trick."

Renton said."I think we will leave it there for now and continue tomorrow."

Back in the collators Frank made Renton and himself a drink while Steve went off to type up the latest interview.

Reg said "So is our boy confessing or hedging his bets?"

Renton said "I think he is of the mind that his quest to avenge the death of his cousin is now complete and he will take his chances accordingly. He is looking at life having just missed the hangman's noose so we shall see. I would still like to talk to him about killing Carlyle which we shall do tomorrow."

Just then in walked Peter with the small case.

"Hello sir."

Renton said "So what have you gleaned from that case and its contents?"

"Well Campbell's fingerprints are on the pouch containing the wire I couldn't get anything off the rolls of money seven hundred pounds to be exact. There was also a small pouch the sort you put a brooch or pendant in." He gave it to Renton. Renton opened it and inside was a single diamond slightly smaller than a golf ball.

Peter said "My uncle works in the jewellery quarter in Sheffield so I rang him and he said that uncut which it is could be worth two thousand pounds but cut and faceted it could be worth a lot more. The passports have his prints on the covers. Also sir that footprint in the bathroom at Crowley's house exactly matches one of Carlyle's shoes."

Renton took the small case and said Reg "Can you lock this in the exhibits locker and we will see what Campbell makes of that. Tomorrow we will have the third interview and will have a short break and then Oskar can swap with Frank but bring in that case. But firstly we will see what he has to say about Horton and then the death of Dekko."

3rd Interview

Once again Renton, Frank and Steve were sitting in the interview room when Campbell was led in by Colin. Renton said "Today is Saturday 16th July 1966" he then went through about solicitors and the caution and who was present.

Renton said "Please read yesterday's interview and if you are satisfied that is a true record then please sign."

Campbell read through it and then signed.

Renton said "Now let's talk about the murder of Gerald Horton, is there anything you would like to say?"

Campbell said "Bonehead Horton the man with no brain but built like a brick outhouse. He certainly had a way with the women and some of the men."

"Horton was part of the plan to kill your cousin Alistair Duggan would you say that is true?"

"He was just carrying out an order from Carlyle but he was just as responsible as far as I was concerned."

"Was Carlyle with you?"

"No he was down in Brighton, shame he wasn't there I could have shown him how to use the wire properly."

"You knew Horton was somewhere in South Elmsall?"

"Yes so I went there and went around a few pubs looking for my old army buddy it didn't take long and then having found him and knowing he liked swinging from both side of the beds I suggested we go somewhere for sex. I made sure he had plenty of drink inside him and said that sex was better outside did he know anywhere. He got in the van and he directed me to a farm I had the club ready because I knew he would put up a fight."

"When you say club you mean a knobkerrie?"

"Haha you bet a fine weapon in the right hands he got out of the van and walked to a stack of hay bales as we got round the back of it I gave him the club on the back of the head he went straight down. I quickly tied his arms and ankles good and tight and then slapped him a few times to wake him which he eventually did I then told him I was going to kill him for what he had done to Al."

"Did you get any response?" Frank said.

"You bet he told me that mummy's boy got his just desserts for being a grass and good riddance that did it I got the wire and snuffed out his life and left him to bleed to death."

Renton said "Righto time for a short break and see you in half an hour."

30 minutes later Renton had Colin take Campbell to the interview room first. Renton Oskar and Steve came in the room and sat down. Renton said "James this is Detective Sergeant Peplinksi."

Campbell looked him up and down but said nothing.

Oskar produced the small case and Renton said "This is exhibit OP/1." He opened the case and said "Here we have a small pouch and it contains this." He pulled out the loop of wire.

"James is this yours?"

Campbell said "Yes everything in that case is mine and so you don't keep on that wire was used to kill the people we have spoken about."

"Tell me about the passports?"

"I got them made up in Berlin, they look pretty convincing don't you think if you have hard cash you can get anything. James Duggan is obvious even to you three. Otto Meier was the German guy who was the head of security for the club and another one he challenged me about my identity out in the street one night, I always carried a small blade so I decided he had to die. I dropped him down a manhole."

Oscar said "So you killed the Gorilla."

As soon as Campbell heard Oskar's voice he said "Aha so Gunter you have grown a beard and now speak perfect English. Otto said he thought you were a plant but I thought it was just him being over cautious."

Renton said "Time for a dinner break and then we will talk about Carlyle."

Campbell was shown back to his cell.

Renton said "I could see him looking you over but as soon as you spoke he knew who you were."

Oscar said "I always wondered who killed Otto he was built like a gorilla for sure. They found his body about a week after he went down there because he was blocking the main sewer."

2pm and they were back in the interview room.

Renton said "So now we come to Carlyle last but not least."

Campbell said "I got the most pleasure out of killing that piece of work I can tell you."

"Did you kill him in the garage or somewhere else?"

"In the garage."

Renton said "So when did Carlyle come back presumably after you killed Horton?"

"He was getting into the antiques big time and said keep the van we can make a few trips and a lot of money. There was this chap in North Yorkshire who had quite a bit of stuff he was willing to sell and Dekko said we could get quite a bit for it but in Brighton. The dealer in Brighton would sell antiques to various clients in the south and in France. We did a few trips down to Brighton and made quite a bit of money. I was biding my time waiting for the chance to do him. I had decided to kill him in the garage. So I had bought this kidney desk in Harrogate and put it in the garage and said to him to have look see what he thought of it. Luckily he had left the Jag in Brighton in a lock up. We got to the garage and he opened the doors and I drove the van in. He closed the two doors. I got out and showed him the desk and he said "You've been had this is a pile of shit Jimmy." He only called me Jimmy when he was being sarcastic. He turned round and I punched him in the face as hard as I could. He went down. I pounced on him and tied his hands together then picked him up and tied his arms and ankles to the chair and gagged him. I had a small bottle of whisky so I just sat there and had a tot or two and waited for him to wake up."

"Oskar said "So what time of day was this?"

"It had to be about 8.30 at night."

"Can you give us a date roughly?"

"I can tell you exactly the date it was the 21st of May because that is a date I will never forget it's the day I joined the Legion in Paris."

Renton looked in his diary and said "A Saturday."

Oskar said "So you have Carlyle all tied up so what happened when he woke up."

"I could see the fear in his eyes he wasn't the bravest person I have ever met. I told him about Al being my cousin and I had waited so long for this moment. I think he had pissed himself by this time. He tried to say something so I punched him several times in the face you know this one is for Al this one is for his dad and this one is for me. I told him I thought about shooting him in the face so he could know the pain that Al had felt. He was mumbling something and I thought what a pathetic creature he was. I got the wire out and dangled it in front of his face but I was raging by this time so I stood behind him and strangled the life out of him it felt so good I cannot describe it as I did him I said "This is for my cousin Alistair. It was like a release of emotion."

"Then what did you do?" said Renton.

I undid him from the chair and then put him on the cardboard I found some sacking and covered him up. I locked up the garage then drove back to the digs had a bath and went to bed. On the Monday I went back put the van in the garage and put him in the van and covered him up with the sacking. I had rented the garage to August so I intended to eventually dispose of the body maybe dig a hole and dump him or maybe in the sea somewhere. I got the train to Brighton I had his keys for the lock up and the Jag. Took the girlfriend away for a week or so in the Jag. She had a friend who had a boat at Shoreham so I was thinking maybe I could give him a watery grave. Then I got arrested for smacking that gobby cop."

Renton said "We will call it a day we will bring in the statement today for you to read and sign and that is about it."

Campbell said "So what happens now."

Renton said "You will be charged with murder of Cooper, Stewart, Horton and Carlyle and being an accessory to the murder of Kowalski. You will appear at Doncaster court and be remanded in custody. Then the file will go to the Attorney General for his consideration and he will set a date for the trial which will probably be at the Old Bailey. If you are found guilty the judge will then sentence you."

"To life in prison I think I would prefer the death sentence." Campbell said.

After Campbell was taken back to his cell Oskar said "Do you get the feeling he knows something that we don't he just doesn't seem the slightest bit bothered."

Renton said "He is a very confident sort."

48
Last Interview

Renton arrived at his office to find no files to be read through and signed up. Ten minutes later he was in the collators enjoying his first coffee of the day.

Reg said "So all dusted and sorted a full confession to the murders I should think the Chief will be well pleased."

Oskar said "Unless of course he refuses to sign the last statement and says you stitched him up."

Frank said "You are such a ray of hope in these trying times Oskar."

Renton said "I will go to morning prayers with you Frank and then tell them what has happened so far and then we will go for the last interview."

One hour later they were sitting in the interview room as Campbell was brought in, Renton reminded him about the caution then gave him the statement to read which he did and then signed it.

Campbell said "What now?"

Renton said "You will be charged tomorrow morning and then taken to the court and then be remanded to prison awaiting trial. Have you anything else to say?"

Campbell said "Well if the Redcaps had done their job properly then that gang of cretins would have been arrested and we wouldn't be sitting here now"

Renton said "But would it have been enough justice for you because they may have only got prison sentences would it have been revenge or justice."

Campbell just shrugged his shoulders and said "Revenge every time."

Campbell was taken back to his cell when he was locked up Renton said to Colin the jailor "How has he been any aggression or change of personality?"

"No sir he has been fine he asked for some reading material so I gave him my Daily Telegraph and a small stub of a pencil to do the cryptic crossword which he did in a hour and then gave me the pencil back."

Renton went to the collators and said "I am calling it a day and I will see you tomorrow Frank if you could type up the charges ready for tomorrow."

It was a 10.10pm Renton was just about to clean his teeth before he went to bed when the telephone rang Jenny answered it then shouted up the stairs "Inspector Walker your star prisoner has attempted suicide."

Renton ran down the stairs and took the receiver

"Inspector Walker nights inspector sorry to ring you at this late hour sir but Campbell has tried to kill himself PC Parkin was about to be relieved by PC Bradley and on every shift changeover we always check the prisoners in their cells they went into the cell and pulled back the blanket to find him covered in blood almost unconscious he is now on his way with them to the hospital who have been forewarned."

Renton said "Can you contact Frank Dipper and I will meet him there."

"Yes sir there is a car on its way to pick you."

Renton turned round and Jenny was standing there with his clothes.

Fifteen minutes later he was in a car he said to the driver Sergeant Ramsden "Do we know how he did it?"

"Some sort of a blade he had kept up his arse."

Several minutes later they arrived at the hospital as he went to the entrance he was met by Frank.

"Bloody hell Frank you didn't hang around?"

"I only live round the corner don't I so what's Campbell done?"

"Jack and Dennis are here we find them we find out what happened."

49
I have washed it

As they walked into the hospital Renton saw a nurse and said "Nurse can you tell me what is happening to a man just brought in an attempted suicide?"

She said in a sarcastic tone "You mean the nearly dead man handcuffed to a stretcher" she emphasized the word handcuffed "he is in the operating theatre."

She turned away and Frank said with a smile "Jack and Dennis do not take any chances even with a nearly dead man."

Just then Jack and Dennis came out of the toilets having cleaned up.

Renton said "Where the hell did he get a blade from?"

Jack said "From up his backside in this." He passed what looked like a small tube to Renton saying "I have washed it boss."

Renton looked at it and pulled the small 3 inch blade out and said "It looks just like a small fountain pen you would never know what is inside." He gave it to Frank who looked at the blade "Rodgers of Sheffield made these during the was my cousin in Sheffield Dorothy was a blade wiper, they cleaned and sharpened them and they then went to another room where the blades were fitted in pens and lighters."

Dennis said "Well it did a good job on his neck."

Jack found a small kitchen and made them a drink and 15 minutes later a doctor came in and said "Your man died several minutes ago he made a good job on his main vein obviously I will certify death and send you a copy. He will be stitched up and taken to our mortuary I don't think you need to have a post mortem but I will ring Doctor Wells to let him know."

Renton said "Righto back to the station for me take a look at the cell and then home for some shuteye and back at 9am to see the Chief."

Twenty minutes later he was looking in the cell and picked up the newspaper written in pencil across the top was "Better to die than spend my life in a ten foot square room." Renton said to the jailer I will take this for the file lock the cell up we will need photographs of it ready for the internal enquiry." Ted Ramsden then took him home.

Coda

8.30am Renton went into the collators and showed them the newspaper with the comment by Campbell written on the top. 9am he went to see the Chief and also showed him the newspaper and what had happened during the night.

Later in the collators he said to Reg "The Chief wants all the team to be here at 1pm so have everyone here 20 minutes before so they can get a drink and then we will see what he has to say. Once the enquiry has finished over the suicide you can contact all the witnesses I will call Mr Duggan. Frank and I will now make up the murder file which will never get to court."

By 1pm everyone was sitting in the incident room having had a drink and finished off the Jammy Dodgers much to the disgust of Reg. The Chief walked in and everyone stood up he beckoned them to sit down and declined a drink.

"I just wanted to say despite the outcome of the suicide of Campbell I would like to commend you all for the sterling work you have done leading up to date. In actual fact you solved the case even though it won't get to court. No matter I am very proud of you all although trying times are ahead. But a new start also as Doncaster will eventually become part of the West Yorkshire Constabulary amalgamating with Barnsley Dewsbury Halifax Huddersfield and Wakefield. The Attorney General has asked us to get out unsolved serious crime cases such as murder of which we have one and attempt to solve or bring them to a proper conclusion. Food for thought thank you."

With that he left again everyone stood up.

Renton then said "I will be in the Red Lion at 6pm and my wallet will be open for exactly ten minutes."
As everyone filed out Reg beckoned to Renton. "Did you notice the Chief mention that we only have one unsolved murder case?

"Yes I thought that a bit strange considering he was giving us a pat on the back."

"Rumour has it that all county forces are being encouraged to solve all murder and serious crimes such as armed robbery. So no rest for the wicked also I had our old friend DS Jackson ring me this morning apparently Carlyle and Campbell deserted from the Legion and are suspect for a bank robbery in Paris."

"Too late." Renton said.

The End.

Printed in Great Britain
by Amazon